THE
SECRET
CELESTIAL
ARCHIVE

ETHAN CROSS

The Secret Celestial Archive

TABLE OF CONTENTS

THE SECRET CELESTIAL ARCHIVE

An ancient heritage awaits discovery in a world where awareness longs to grow. The fabled Eldari civilization produced the Secret Celestial Archive, which symbolizes the potential to alter consciousness more than just information. The Archive contains secrets that might drastically change how sentient creatures see and interact with reality; they have been lost to time and are shielded by trials meant to test knowledge rather than power.

Into this cosmic mystery steps Lena Chen, a brilliant archaeologist whose disillusionment with traditional academia masks a deeper understanding of ancient mysteries. When she discovers a cryptic tablet bearing Eldari script, her passion for discovery is reignited, along with her connection to her past—particularly the mysterious disappearance of her grandfather during an expedition years ago. The tablet is more than just an artifact; it is a key to unlocking the potential for consciousness evolution.

Lena goes to Kai, a technical genius whose skills blur the boundaries between human and machine awareness, after realizing the gravity of her discovery. He has a unique perspective on the perils of the Shadow Consortium because of his enigmatic background with this influential group, which aims to impose evolution rather than acquire it through knowledge. Together, they unlock the secrets of the tablet and inadvertently produce patterns in reality that trigger an action from the Archive.

Dr. Elara, a well-known astrophysicist whose sharp intellect belies nuanced reasons, joins them in their partnership. Her deep understanding of cosmic ideas makes her a useful partner, but her secret ties to the Shadow Consortium sow the seeds for future strife. The three viewpoints—scientific knowledge, technical insight, and archaeological wisdom—create a resonance that profoundly influences how reality reacts to their presence.

Every place they visit offers difficulties that test their skills and knowledge of evolution. The crystalline wastes of Frostholm force them to face the real cost of metamorphosis, while the Temple of Echoes on Veridia presents them with rifts in vision. As they progress, they understand that the Archive is a living system intended to direct the growth of consciousness by acquired wisdom rather than coerced authority.

The Shadow Consortium's unrelenting pursuit of its objective shows the immense risks associated with it. This influential group uses quantum consciousness experiments that threaten the fundamental foundation of existence by spreading corruption across reality because they feel that humanity's transformation cannot wait for natural growth.

When Dr. Elara's true allegiance is revealed, betrayal catalyzes a deeper understanding of evolution. Her attempt to force evolution through the Archive's power underscores a fundamental difference: transformation earned through wisdom versus power seized through force. The primary conflict of the story, which involves a struggle for control of the Archive as well as a thorough examination of the appropriate development of consciousness, is initiated by this discovery.

Our heroes encounter Professor Jin along the journey. His research on the evolution of consciousness provides important clues about the Archive's nature. They learn that the Archive, created by the Eldari to help other species progress naturally, is more than simply a repository of information; it is a portal to higher levels of awareness.

After the story, our protagonists are forced to make a crucial decision. Their experiences have increased their awareness, allowing them to see reality in previously unimaginable ways. They have to decide whether to protect the Archive and advance to this special blend of awareness, which creates fresh opportunities for change and shows how evolution may strengthen bonds while overcoming constraints.

The last encounter with the Shadow Consortium shows divergent views on development and develops into more than simply a struggle for dominance. Through their acquired understanding, Lena, Kai, and their comrades demonstrate that real power comes from harmonizing with existence rather than forcing change. They must change rather than destroy to overcome the corruption brought about by forced evolution.

Ultimately, The Secret Celestial Archive becomes a story about awareness itself, moving beyond its beginnings as a discovery story. Through the experiences of its protagonists, the story demonstrates the distinction between wisdom and knowledge, demonstrating that genuine power originates from understanding rather than dominance. It implies that evolution may enhance ties rather than necessitate their sacrifice.

The story closes with a new beginning rather than a finish as our characters come to terms with their positions as intermediaries between various levels of consciousness. They teach future generations that true change comes from having the courage to evolve in harmony with the natural environment rather than by force, and they also demonstrate how evolution may strengthen ties while bridging barriers.

Like the Eldari before them, their legacy becomes crucial to how reality permits the development of consciousness. It emphasizes that rather than attempting to control the world, the way to true understanding is to become more conscious of where one is in it. *The Secret Celestial Archive* demonstrates the power of information gained, the strength of collective consciousness, and the boundless potential for development by understanding rather than force.

INTRODUCTION
THE HIDDEN LEGACY

Numerous civilizations have risen and gone like waves on an endless beach in the immense fabric of cosmic history. But in myth and recollection, one planet sticks out: Elysium. This planet, synonymous with the heights of consciousness evolution, emerged during the twilight of what scholars now term the First Age of Understanding.

Elysium was more than a beacon of knowledge; it was a testament to what consciousness could achieve through wisdom rather than force. The civilization that flourished there discovered a profound truth: reality is an expression of consciousness, and true power comes not from controlling existence but from understanding one's place within it.

At the heart of their society stood the Secret Celestial Archive, a term woefully inadequate for the living entity it represented. Housed within crystalline structures that defied conventional physics, this Archive preserved information, experiences, understanding, and the essence of evolved consciousness.

The halls of the Archive stretched across multiple dimensions, with crystalline shelves existing simultaneously in physical space and realms of pure thought. Each artifact, scroll, and tome was a key to understanding reality's deeper nature—windows into states of consciousness that most beings could scarcely imagine.

Instead of just imparting information, researchers who visited Elysium found that the Archive responded to the consciousness of its visitors. The crystalline shelves would move as they demonstrated their readiness, forming knowledge routes corresponding to each seeker's capacity for learning. Because of this dynamic involvement, the Archive is unique as a living manual for pursuing knowledge.

However, the Archive's true purpose extended beyond knowledge preservation. It was a means of guiding the development of consciousness itself. The Eldari, the people of Elysium, recognized that consciousness could evolve beyond its current limitations but only through wisdom rather than force. Their goal was not merely to create a knowledge repository but to offer a pathway for authentic evolution—a resonance that would guide others toward transformation.

With such power came profound responsibility. The Eldari were aware that if utilized improperly, the power to affect the development of awareness may have disastrous results. As a result, they included protections into the Archive's structure to guarantee that it would only react to those who approached it with knowledge rather than a desire for control. Roached it with genuine understanding rather than a lust for power.

When ancient seers foresaw the cataclysm threatening their civilization, they recognized it as more than a physical disaster. It represented a critical point in consciousness evolution—a moment requiring society to choose between clinging to physical existence and evolving into something outside of everyday reality.

In response, the High Council met in an area between dimensions where awareness could see the actual patterns of reality rather than in a physical chamber. Their conversations went beyond simple conversation to become a harmonic manifestation of their advanced consciousness, looking for the best course of action.

Their solution was elegant and profound: rather than hiding the Archive, they would transform it into the fabric of reality itself. The barrier they created was not merely a shield but a series of trials and tests designed to ensure that only those who understood the true nature of consciousness evolution could access the Archive's deeper secrets.

As the Council spoke the final incantations—patterns of thought that reshaped quantum reality—they encoded their civilization's most profound insights into the Archive's structure: that true power lies not in controlling reality but in growing harmoniously within existence itself.

The transformation of the Archive was observed across multiple dimensions of reality. Physical observers saw it shimmer and fade from normal space, while those with evolved consciousness perceived its integration into deeper layers of existence. The Archive had not merely been hidden—it had become integral to the evolution of consciousness itself.

In addition to destroying Elysium's physical civilization, the apocalypse sparked Eldari's ultimate metamorphosis, enabling those prepared to advance beyond everyday life. Some choose to stay on as guides, becoming a part of the Archive's structure and its goal to support its future development.

The ruins of Elysium became mere shadows of the civilization that had transcended physical limitations. Yet, the Archive endured—not only hidden but transformed, waiting for consciousness to grow and rediscover it.

The Archive's influence subtly shaped reality throughout eons of cosmic time while younger civilizations rose and fell. It became more than its creators intended—not just a repository of wisdom but a living testament to the potential of consciousness evolving through understanding rather than force.

The Archive awaited discovery, not in patience or impatience, but within the eternal now of evolved awareness. It would be found when beings emerged who understood that true power comes not from seizing knowledge but from harmonizing with existence itself.

Thus, Elysium's legacy persisted—not merely as legend or myth but as a quantum possibility waiting to manifest. It represented a doorway to evolution that would open only when consciousness learned to approach it through wisdom instead of force.

The Archive's story preserves knowledge and protects the evolution of true consciousness, showing future beings that understanding, not control, can bring about transformation. The Archive is hidden deep within reality, waiting to be found and to lead those ready to evolve into greater harmony with existence.

Rediscovery was imminent, but not in the way everyone had anticipated. The Archive's impact had subtly prepared reality, offering consciousness a glimpse of possibilities it had not yet contemplated. A new chapter in the amazing journey of growth was about to begin.

CHAPTER

1

SECRETS UNVEILED

The ancient stone chamber held its breath, and dust motes danced in the beam of Lena's lantern, catching the light like tiny stars in the oppressive darkness. Her fingers trembled—not from fear, but from the electric anticipation coursing through her veins. After fifteen years of searching, countless dead ends, and false leads, she might finally have found something real.

In front of her was a tablet unlike any she had ever seen while working in archaeology. Its surface was covered with markings that were hard to classify, with symbols that varied and developed according to the angle of view. The most intriguing aspect was the elaborate map carved into its center; it was a network of lines and nodes that, by comparison, made her father's complex mathematics seem simple.

"Oh, you beautiful thing," she whispered, barely breaking the long stillness. "What secrets are you hiding?"

Lena noticed a slight iridescence on its surface as her lantern's beam illuminated the stone more fully. This wasn't merely carved but engineered, featuring microscopic structures that altered with the angle of light. It was advanced technology beyond anything in the archaeological record.

With careful and accurate motions, she reached inside her bag for scanning equipment. Years spent at dangerous dig sites, where one mistake may ruin valuable artifacts, had taught her the need for patience. Her hands, however, continued to shake. If she were correct, the tablet's provenance would alter everything.

The scanner's soft blue light danced across the surface, gathering data that would take weeks to analyze properly. But Lena couldn't wait that long; she needed to know now. The symbols on the tablet's edge caught her eye—fragments she had seen in restricted archives and forbidden collections. Eldari script.

The name sent her heart racing. The Eldari were an enigmatic civilization that vanished at the height of its power, leaving behind only whispers of their existence and legends of a Celestial Archive— a repository of knowledge that could dwarf humanity's understanding of the cosmos.

To many archaeologists, the Archive was a fairy tale recounted to wide-eyed students yearning for the next big find. But Lena had amassed too much evidence and spotted too many connections to dismiss it as a legend. The tablet before she bore the same mathematical precision and impossible properties as other confirmed Eldari artifacts. But this was different; it wasn't just another piece of their technology but a map.

The scanner's beep brought her back to the present. Its first analysis left her gasping for air. Normal physics could not produce the crystal lattices that could only be achieved in traditional Eldari engineering, and the nature of the material was unknown. More significantly, the scan uncovered data concealed behind the tablet's exterior. This topographical map had mathematical formulas, spatial and chronological coordinates, and what seemed to be security measures. It was a key, not only a route to a place.

With her mind racing, Lena slumped back on her heels. She became overwhelmed by the intricacy of the math and knew she needed assistance. Uncovering security measures and the tablet's secrets would require experience—someone adept at navigating the physical and virtual labyrinths that concealed the Archive from curious eyes.

Kai, was that someone?

The idea was enticing, causing a mixture of fear and excitement. Perhaps the greatest coder and hacker she had ever met, Kai was a genius. However, he was also violent, erratic, and plagued by mysteries she had never entirely comprehended. But he was the one who could assist her in solving the riddles of the tablet.

She covered the tablet in a protective cloth and tucked it inside her reinforced case with gentle reverence. It seemed like fate that the weight was on her back. With each step she took toward the surface, she was getting closer to the future she had long hoped to discover, which carried new risks, opportunities, and questions.

The compartment was too well-preserved and concealed to be a mere coincidence. The right person at the right time had sought after this pill. As Lena navigated the tight passageways that would eventually lead her back to the surface, she felt an unsettling presence, as if history itself was watching her. It wasn't the old rooms that made her nervous—the scan had ensured no surveillance devices in this forgotten place. The Eldari's preparations indicated that someone would follow the trail before her.

However, others were watching as well.

As she approached the door, she heard the first sign that something was amiss—a whisper that didn't belong to the settling stone and a shadow that shouldn't have been there. Lena's training kicked in, prompting her to freeze. She remembered the mantra: Plan, observe, listen.

The shadow shifted again, this time with purpose. Whoever was there made a concerted effort to remain unseen and undetected—certainly not careless locals or casual treasure seekers. This presence signaled something far more dangerous.

Her mind raced through the possibilities. Lena knew these ruins better than anyone, yet she also understood the main entrance was likely guarded. After months of meticulous surveying, she discovered a collapsed passage and revealed a connection to a parallel tunnel system. But escaping through there would require time, something she might not have.

A refined, exacting voice drifted through the rooms: "Doctor Chen? I believe you have something that belongs to us."

Lena's blood froze. The well-known astrophysicist Dr. Elara's voice was all too familiar. How did she know what Lena had found, and why was she here?

Lena's immediate objective was to survive; she couldn't afford to ponder questions. Silently and confidently, she turned into a side tunnel. One advantage she had was their ignorance of her knowledge about the escape routes—and, more importantly, their lack of awareness about Kai's presence.

Her thoughts raced as she made her way through the dimly lit hallways. She needed to secure the tablet, contact Kai, and understand Dr. Elara's involvement. Above all, she had to safeguard what could be the most significant archaeological find in human history.

With every step, the tablet's weight pressed heavily against her back, its secrets searing into her mind like fire. The Eldari had created their Archive to safeguard knowledge, confining it until

4

humanity was ready. Now, that same knowledge required protection anew.

Lena allowed herself a grim smile as she slipped through the collapsed section of the tunnel. Let them search the main chambers; she would be halfway to Kai's hideout when they realized she was gone. And then, the real work would begin. This was the final call in the search for the Celestial Archive, and nothing—not even the most formidable obstacles—would stand in her way.

Above the chaos of New Shanghai's tech district, forty stories up, Kai sat in his apartment, enveloped by the soft hum of servers and the gentle glow of holographic displays. His fingers danced across haptic interfaces, weaving effortlessly through security systems.

He was testing a new firewall belonging to a major quantum research facility, hired through layers of deniability to probe its defenses. So far, he has identified three critical vulnerabilities. However, something about the fourth layer of security bothered him; the code was too elegant, too perfect—almost as if it were designed not just to protect but to deceive.

Suddenly, his big screen flashed red: an intrusion detection alert. This wasn't part of the facility's security measures; it was entirely different. Someone was attempting to hack into his systems.

A grin pulled at his mouth's corners. He said, "Amateur hour," as his fingertips flitted over the interfaces. It was a clever but predictable assault strategy he had seen many times before. When he traced the attack to its origin, he discovered something odd: the hacker aimed to compromise his building's security cameras rather than his primary systems.

The moment became more urgent. Someone was observing him, but why? He had to go quickly.

The smile had vanished. He was no longer alone.

A glance at the external feeds confirmed his unease: three men in unremarkable business attire stood around the main entrance of the

5

building. Their stance shouted military, and the shapes beneath their jackets hinted at a troubling narrative he wasn't prepared to confront.

Kai activated his emergency protocols. Drives began self-erasing, backups transferred to secure locations, and false trails sprawled across the network like digital breadcrumbs. He had learned long ago that the best defense wasn't just about good security and an escape plan.

Suddenly, the soft chime of his private comm channel cut through his concentration.

"Kai," a familiar voice said, urgent and breathless.

"Lena? It's been what, two years?"

"I found it, Kai. I found it."

Something in her tone sent a chill down his spine; Lena Chen knew how to uncover the extraordinary. The last time she had called like this; she'd uncovered evidence of advanced quantum computing in ancient ruins. But this felt different. She sounded terrified.

"Where are you?" he asked, his heart racing.

"Two blocks from your place, in the old subway station. I'm being followed."

Kai's screens shifted, pulling up camera feeds from the abandoned station. Although the technology down there was deteriorating, he had supplemented it with his sensors. "I see them," he said, noting the three professionals in military gear disguised as civilians. "They're a different group from the ones watching my building."

"There's more of them?"

"It looks like we're both popular tonight." He studied the thermal scans. "Take the maintenance tunnel on your left. It'll lead you to the service elevator in Building 23. I can get you up here without being seen."

"Kai." Lena hesitated; her voice laced with tension. "This is bigger than anything we've dealt with before. Are you sure about this?"

He glanced at the screens surrounding him, eyes tracking the ordered movements of the teams hunting them both. These weren't ordinary mercenaries or corporate security—they were entirely different.

"Just like old times, right?" Kai's attempt at humor fell flat, his mind racing with escape plans and contingencies. "Get moving. And Lena? Keep an eye on the third junction. The sensor has been misbehaving.

His fingertips skimmed over the controls as they made their way through the subterranean labyrinth. False signals led their pursuers in circles, door locks clicked open and closed precisely, and security cameras flashed in loops. He was an expert at this digital dance of power and deceit.

But something didn't feel quite correct. The timing couldn't have been more ideal—attacks on both occurred simultaneously with Lena's revelation. Everything about this occasion appeared to have been prearranged.

A few seconds later, his lift hummed to life. He had constructed it with military-grade stealth technology and sufficient protection against a small army. The doors gently slid open as Lena stood at the entryway. Although she had a tired expression, her eyes scanned the room and carefully examined his barriers.

"Nice setup," she remarked, stepping inside. "Very paranoid."

"Says the woman being chased by a tactical team," Kai replied with a smirk, gesturing toward a secure workstation. "Show me what was worth bringing this down on our heads."

Lena carefully retrieved a reinforced case from her pack. Her reverence as she handled it told Kai that this wasn't just another artifact but something significant.

As she unfurled the protective wrapping, Kai's screens flickered—just a brief glitch, barely perceptible to anyone else, yet it sent an adrenaline rush through him. Even though the tablet within was unplugged and unpowered, its existence interfered with his systems.

"That can't be," he leaned closer and whispered. The marks carved on the tablet's surface seemed to move, settling into designs that moved in ways he couldn't comprehend.

At that moment, he realized that they were not just playing cat and mouse—they were players in a far more dangerous chess match, with lives hanging in the balance.

"It gets better." Lena powered up her scanner, transferring the preliminary data to his system. "Look at the internal structure."

As the analysis flooded his displays, Kai's eyes became wide. The tablet's crystalline matrix was more complex than anything he had ever seen. Information was being processed and evolved in addition to being stored.

"This is Eldari tech," he said in a low voice, almost amazed. "Actual, confirmed Eldari technology."

"Not just technology." A mixture of anxiety and exhilaration glistened in Lena's eyes. Kai, it's a map. The Archive's map.

The words hung between them, thick with both possibility and danger. If Lena was correct, this tablet could lead them to the Celestial Archive, the greatest repository of knowledge ever created, which had been lost for millennia.

A soft alarm pulsed on one of his secondary screens. "We've got company," he said, activating the external feeds. "Multiple teams converging on the building—professional gear, military coordination." He zoomed in on one of the figures. "And our friend Dr. Elara is with them."

Lena's expression hardened. "How do they have someone like her working for them? She's one of the most respected astrophysicists in the field."

"Everyone has secrets." Kai's fingers flew across the interface as he initiated more aggressive countermeasures. "The question is, what makes this tablet worth exposing them?"

"It's not just the tablet." Lena's voice was quiet yet intense. "It's what it leads to. The Archive. It's real, Kai. All the stories and legends about the Eldari and their knowledge are real. And someone is willing to kill to control it."

Kai examined the tablet, noting the complexity of the security systems. Hacking into something like this wouldn't be easy. It would demand all his skills, and he'd probably have to improvise.

"How long do you need?" Lena asked, gauging his expression.

"To crack Eldari security that's been evolving for thousands of years?" He allowed himself a grim smile. "Better make some coffee. This is going to take a while."

A deeper alarm blared—a proximity warning. Their pursuers were in the building.

"Time, we don't have," Lena said, checking her gear. "Can you work on the move?"

Kai was already gathering his valuable equipment, moving quickly and methodically. "The security on that tablet is unlike anything I've ever seen. It's not just complicated—it's alive. Adaptive. I'll need specialized equipment and a secure location."

"The university lab?"

"Too obvious. They'll look there first." He paused, weighing their options. "I know a place—off the grid and shielded from scanning. But getting there won't be easy."

Lena secured the tablet in its case. "It never is."

9

The building shook as security teams began breaching the lower levels. Kai's screens displayed their methodical advance, sweeping through each floor with military precision. They had ten minutes before they reached their level.

"Remember that job in Singapore?" he asked, activating his emergency evacuation protocols. "The one with the quantum prototype?"

Lena's eyes widened. "Please tell me you're not suggesting—"

"Same principle, different tech." He gestured toward the window—the maintenance cradle attached to the building's exterior. "Sometimes the best way to avoid high-tech security is to go low-tech."

"You're insane," Lena replied, but she was already moving towards the window. "You know that, right?"

"Sanity's overrated." Kai sealed his portable drives and slung his bag over his shoulder. "Besides, you're the one who showed up at my door with lost alien technology and a tactical team on your tail."

The building's security alerts multiplied as teams moved swiftly across multiple floors. It would take eight minutes—maybe less—before they arrived.

"When we survive this," Lena said, stepping onto the cradle, "we need to have a serious discussion about your definition of a backup plan."

Kai's fingers flew over the cradle's ancient controls, plotting their descent. "When we survive this, we'll be too busy cracking the greatest technological mystery in human history."

The cradle jerked and began to move. Above them, breach charges detonated across Kai's floor, while below them, forty stories of open air, drenched with rain and aglow with the city's neon lights, awaited.

Somewhere out there, the Archive lay hidden, its secrets beckoning to them like a siren. All they had to do was survive long enough to uncover it.

Dr. Elara stood in Kai's abandoned apartment; her expression icy as she surveyed the suddenly vacant space. Holographic displays flickered with dying programs, their light casting eerie shadows upon the walls. The hum of cooling servers mingled with the soft patter of rain against the windowpanes.

"Report," she said in a quiet, authoritative voice, bearing the weight of authority that made her feared and respected in the scientific world.

One of her agents moved forward, wearing tactical gear that stood out against the tech-heavy décor of the flat. They departed almost seven minutes ago. The surveillance feeds are disrupted, but the building sensors indicate activity on the maintenance cradle.

Elara turned toward the window, watching the rain form patterns on the glass. Years of maintaining a spotless scientific reputation had led to this moment. The Celestial Archive was not merely an archaeological find but a key to powers beyond human imagination.

"Predictable," she muttered, peering through the rain-soaked lens into the distance. "Lena's improvisational skills are impressive but ultimately limited by her moral compass." She turned to her team. "Deploy the drones. Conduct full-spectrum scanning. They can't have gone far."

Elara's gaze fell upon Kai's main workstation as her orders were carried out. Even in his haste, he had meticulously cleaned his systems. Then something caught her eye. Leaning closer, she noticed a subtle pattern in the decay rate of the holographic displays.

"Interesting choice, Kai," she whispered. The pattern was not random but a plain-sighted message—the kind of arrogance a true genius would display. He wanted them to follow.

11

"Ma'am," another operative said, drawing her attention. "We're detecting residual energy signatures. The tablet was here."

Elara nodded, unfazed. "The Eldari device would have left traces; their technology never truly powers down." Her fingers brushed over the holographic displays. "What matters is the data Lena transferred to his systems. Even if wiped, there will be echoes."

Her team worked efficiently with specialized scanning equipment developed secretly by the Shadow Consortium. They had been preparing for this moment for decades; honing tools designed to track and contain Eldari technology.

A soft ping from her neural implant signaled an incoming message. "Report."

"Ground teams have identified their likely exit path," a voice informed her. They're moving east, taking cover through the old commercial district."

Elara said, "Keep back but don't lose them," She walked up to the apartment's security console and ran her fingertips over the screen. "Forward containment units to these coordinates." In front of her, a map sprang to life, showing important junctions. "They'll need a secure location to look at the tablet. Let's restrict their choices.

Elara smiled a little to herself. Lena and Kai were intelligent in their own right, but they had no idea how big of a mess they had fallen into. The Archive was more than simply a storehouse of information; it was a weapon, a control mechanism with the power to alter civilization.

"Ma'am," yelled one of her techs. We have successfully recovered a portion of his quantum buffer's data. They extracted data from the tablet's internal structure.

"Show me," she said back.

The screen flickered to life, revealing complex crystalline patterns that pulsed with impossible symmetry. Eldari engineering was more beautiful and terrifying than anything humanity had achieved. The tablet was not merely a map but a key designed to test its holders and determine if they were worthy of the Archive's power.

"How much did they decode?" Elara asked, studying the patterns.

"Preliminary analysis only," the technician fumbled. "But there's an indication that the tablet responded to them. The security protocols initiated an appraisal sequence."

Elara's expression hardened. If it had accepted them as potential candidates, retrieval would be significantly more complicated. Eldari security systems were notoriously deadly to non-users.

"Expand the search perimeter," she ordered. "Full-spectrum monitoring. I want every camera, every sensor in the city looking for them." She turned to her tactical commander. "Prepare the special containment units. If they've bonded with the tablet, we will need more refined means of persuasion."

Outside, the rain pounded, washing away any evidence of their prey. But Elara wasn't worried. This city was a labyrinth of wires, where every appliance served as a potential surveillance camera, each system an obvious trap. Lena and Kai knew a little; they were dabbling in her world now. In her mind's ear, she heard a chime signaling new developments.

"The ground team reports signs of quantum disturbance," a voice called. "Sector 7 matches active Eldari tech."

"The tablet's stirring," Elara whispered, realization dawning. "It's reacting to their touch." Her mind was made up. "Lock down the sector. Initiate full electromagnetic containment. If the tablet is powering up, it will try to contact other Eldari systems. We can use that to our advantage."

Elara took a moment to consider her next move as her teams mobilized. Centuries of waiting and careful accumulation of power and knowledge by the Shadow Consortium had been aimed at preparing for the moment the Archive would be discovered. She wouldn't let two talented yet naive idealists ruin everything.

"Prepare my private transport," she commanded. "And contact our assets in the quantum research facility. I want to know immediately if they attempt to analyze the tablet through official channels."

The rain thickened, obscuring the city's neon in rivulets of water. Lena and Kai were out there somewhere, carrying technology they could never hope to understand. Yet it would ultimately lead them to what she sought—the Archive itself.

"The game begins," Elara whispered to the rain-dark city. "Let's see how well you play it."

Far away, the rumble of thunder reverberated across the sky, nature's war drums. The hunt for the Celestial Archive had begun in earnest, and the fate of human knowledge hung in the balance. The next moves would determine who found the Archive and who would control the very future of human understanding.

The night was young, yet the secrets of the Eldari were so close. It would be only a matter of following the breadcrumbs that History had left behind for them and eliminating anyone who dared stand in their way.

CHAPTER

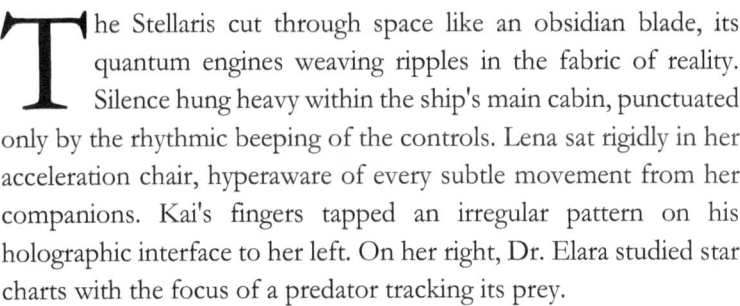

2

THE HEROIC QUEST

The Stellaris cut through space like an obsidian blade, its quantum engines weaving ripples in the fabric of reality. Silence hung heavy within the ship's main cabin, punctuated only by the rhythmic beeping of the controls. Lena sat rigidly in her acceleration chair, hyperaware of every subtle movement from her companions. Kai's fingers tapped an irregular pattern on his holographic interface to her left. On her right, Dr. Elara studied star charts with the focus of a predator tracking its prey.

They had formed an uneasy partnership in the pandemonium of their flight from New Shanghai. They were forced to accept Elara's transportation offer as the Shadow Consortium's soldiers drew closer. Their only way off the planet was her spacecraft, but as Lena watched Elara's strategic maneuvers, she couldn't help but think they could have leaped from one trap to another.

"Approaching the Veridia system," the ship's AI announced, its voice modulated to sound helpful rather than artificial. "Atmospheric entry in seventeen minutes."

Elara's approach vector was adjusted as her fingers moved over the panel. "The Temple of Echoes is situated in the equatorial area. Three km from our destination, there is a clearing, but a straight landing is not feasible due to the forest canopy.

Kai said, "How convenient that you know exactly where we're going," in a sardonic tone. "Almost like you've been planning this."

There was no warmth in Elara's grin. "I've dedicated my whole life to learning about the Eldari. Their temples are designed according to certain patterns, which are mathematical constants.

"And you just happened to crack these patterns on your own?" Kai pushed.

Lena replied, "Kai," seeing the danger in Elara's eyes. "Not now." They needed Elara's expertise, but she understood and shared his concerns. Veridia had been on the ancient tablet, but navigating the planet's dense woods would have been difficult without precise coordinates.

The seriousness of their work weighed hard on the crew as the spacecraft raced towards its goal. The search for the Celestial Archive, entwined with the secrets of the Eldari, was more than just a quest; it was a race against time and crafty opponents. In spite of the brewing suspicion, they would have to rely on one another.

The ship shuddered as it breached the outer atmosphere, plasma streams painting the viewports in brilliant sheets of blue fire. Lena tightened her grip on the armrests, her heart racing. She'd always dreaded atmospheric entry; too many variables and too many ways for things to go wrong.

To distract herself, she broke the tense silence. "The Temple of Echoes. What do we know about it?"

Elara, her tone shifting to the measured cadence of a lecturer, replied, "It's one of seven major Eldari sites discovered in this sector. The architecture suggests it was built approximately twelve thousand years ago during their middle period. Its primary function appears to have been astronomical observation, but like most Eldari structures, it serves multiple purposes."

Kai's skepticism was palpable. "Including hiding keys to their ultimate repository of knowledge?"

Elara said steadily, "The Eldari didn't think as we do." Their information processing techniques and technologies were essentially unlike. They implanted things rather than hiding them. Every building and artifact belonged to a bigger system.

Lena was in awe at the scenery as the ship emerged from the cloud cover. Endless jungles stretched to the horizon, a sea of emerald and gold punctuated by massive tree structures that dwarfed Earth's tallest skyscrapers. Bioluminescent patterns pulsed through the canopy like neural networks, and floating islands of vegetation drifted gracefully on invisible currents, their antigravity properties defying conventional physics.

"Veridia," Elara announced. "One of the few planets where Eldari terraforming remains active. The entire ecosystem is engineered, self-regulating, and possibly sentient."

Kai examined his screens, his brows furrowing. "These readings can't be right. The biological complexity is off the charts."

Lena recalled texts she had studied. "The Eldari didn't just build temples; they grew them. Their technology was a fusion of organic and artificial components."

The ship descended toward a clearing that pulsed with its inner light. Lena realized the ground was alive as they got closer—a massive living platform created by intertwined roots and crystalline structures.

"The landing pad is stable," Elara assured them, noting their concerned expressions. "The crystal matrix maintains its structural integrity through quantum entanglement. We won't sink into the jungle."

The Stellaris touched down with barely a tremor, its landing struts adapting effortlessly to the living surface beneath. Outside, the air was thick with glowing spores that shimmered like starlight, creating a surreal atmosphere.

"Atmospheric analysis shows high oxygen content but no harmful compounds," Elara reported while checking her instruments. "We can breathe normally, but I recommend using full-spectrum filters. Some local flora has intriguing defense mechanisms."

As they prepared their gear, Lena couldn't shake the nagging feeling they were being observed. Not by anything hostile—at least, not yet—but by the jungle itself. The bioluminescent patterns in the vegetation shifted in response to their movements as if the environment were a vast neural network processing new information.

"That way, the temple is three kilometers." Elara pointed to an area of dense vegetation. "If we don't encounter any ... issues, we should get there before dark."

"What complications?" Kai asked, inspecting his tech equipment again.

Elara said, "The ecosystem of Veridia is built to safeguard Eldari sites." "The jungle serves as a defense mechanism, posing challenges and trials to anyone attempting to enter the temples."

"Trials?" Lena's interest in archaeology sparked her interest. "What sort of trials?"

For the first time, Elara's eyes glowed with true joy as she smiled. That is the intriguing aspect. They are flexible. Depending on who tries to go to the temple, the difficulties vary. The Eldari believed that only those who demonstrated their value should have access to knowledge.

As if in response to her words, the jungle ahead shifted, paths appearing and disappearing as the vegetation rearranged itself. Floating spores swirled into patterns that almost resembled writing before dissolving into chaos.

"Well," Kai said, checking his weapon to sound nonchalant, "at least it won't be boring."

They set out into the living maze, each step taking them deeper into one of the most complex ecosystems ever engineered. The first key to unlocking the mysteries of the Celestial Archive was at the Temple of Echoes, which was waiting for them. Lena, however, couldn't eliminate the thought that there would be terrible repercussions for failing if the forest itself evaluated their deservingness. She suspected the solution was ingrained in this old location's DNA.

The jungle presented its first challenge without warning. One moment, they followed a clear path; the next, crystalline structures erupted from the ground in complex geometric patterns, their surfaces reflecting and refracting light in impossible ways.

"Don't move," Elara commanded, studying the formation. "It's a logic gate. One wrong step and the defense systems will activate."

Kai examined the pattern as his scanners buzzed. It processes information and reflects light, and quantum computers are these crystals.

Lena's background in archaeology came into play. "The Eldari were against the idea of distinct systems. Everything was built with several uses and was interrelated. She bent down to look at the closest crystal. "These aren't just barriers; they're reading us, analyzing our approach to problem-solving."

Inner light surged through the crystals, creating patterns that changed like living math. Kai's fingertips skimmed across his portable interface to decipher the reasoning.

"It's a sequence," he replied, putting it together. "Each crystal represents a state in a quantum equation. We must cross in a way that concurrently meets every feasible state. We must cross in an order that satisfies all possible states simultaneously."

"Impossible," Elara stated, disbelief creeping into her voice. "The number of potential combinations—"

"Is infinite," Kai finished a light igniting in his eyes. "Unless... we're thinking about it wrong. The Eldari didn't view mathematics like we do; they saw it as music, as art."

Lena stepped closer to the pattern, seeing it anew. "Look at how the light moves through the crystals. It's not random; it's harmonic. Like sound waves."

"Or brain waves," Elara added, her scientific curiosity momentarily overriding her reserved manner. "The pattern matches theta wave frequencies associated with problem-solving and intuitive thinking."

Kai adjusted his scanners to check for resonance in the pattern. "If we match our movements to the harmonic frequency..."

"We become part of the equation," Lena said, demonstrating her comprehension of the idea. "We are not trying to solve it, but participating in it."

They danced in one as they stepped between the crystals in a purposeful dance that reflected the patterns of the pouring light. In response, the formation shifted its frequency to match their motions and hummed. Only a faint glimmer indicated their journey as the crystals sunk into the earth upon reaching the other side.

"One test down," Kai said as he examined his apparatus. "How many more to go?"

"The temple will continue challenging us until it determines our worthiness," Elara replied. "Each test will be different, probing various aspects of our capabilities and character."

As if responding to Lena's words, the jungle ahead shifted. Massive vines moved like living cables, weaving into intricate bridges and barriers. Bioluminescent spores filled the air, arranging themselves into complex three-dimensional maps.

"The temple's showing us the way," Lena realized. "But not directly. We must solve each section to reveal the next part of the path."

They pressed on, facing increasingly complex challenges. First, a ravine could only be crossed by redistributing quantum energy through a living conductor network. Then, they encountered a maze of light and shadow, where reality folded and unfolded based on their perspectives. Finally, they arrived at a field of crystalline flowers that reacted to their emotional states, requiring perfect harmony among the three travelers to allow passage.

Despite their mutual hatred, Lena saw how successfully they worked together. Elara's extensive understanding of Eldari's science was helpful, while Kai's technical skills improved her archaeological discoveries. It seemed almost too wonderful to be true, like pieces of a jigsaw created just for them.

"The temple's close," Elara said as they finished yet another assignment. "These spore patterns are getting more organized and concentrated."

When the forest canopy started to thin, massive crystalline spires towered into the sky. The Temple of Echoes lived true to its name; each sound that came back changed and carried hints of ancient wisdom.

As she marveled at the temple's organic construction, Lena said, "It's beautiful." Over millennia, living crystal and synthetic life had developed together to form an organismic and structural structure.

"And heavily defended," Kai added, scanning the area. "The security systems are more complex than anything we've encountered."

Elara stepped forward, her expression unreadable. "The outer challenges were just preliminary screening. The real tests begin inside the temple."

As they approached the entrance—a soaring arch that seemed to be made of frozen light—symbols scrolled across its surface in endless patterns, each holding meanings that could take lifetimes to decode.

"The inscription," Lena translated, running her fingers over the symbols. "It says: 'Knowledge is transformation. Enter as you are, leave as you must become.'"

Kai mumbled, "Cryptic," yet his voice had a touch of gratitude for the engineering.

As they crossed the threshold, the temples inside illumination reacted to their arrival. Crystal and living metal corridors extended in all directions, each buzzing at its frequency.

Elara said, "The orb will be in the central chamber," with unexpected certainty. "These corridors are meant to prepare us for its power."

"How do you know so much about this place?" Kai asked, suspicion creeping back. "Even the most detailed archaeological records don't have this level of specific information."

Elara had a mysterious grin. "Mr. Chen, knowledge may take many different forms, and official records do not contain all of them.

The temple itself stepped in before Kai could push any farther. A huge mechanism that ran through the temple's foundations was visible as the floor beneath them changed, turning transparent. Like blood through arteries, energy pulsed through crystalline veins, leading to a central location.

"The temple's center," Lena realized. "That's where we'll find the orb."

But reaching it would prove to be their greatest challenge yet.

The temple's internal defenses were unlike anything they had encountered in the jungle. Rooms were rearranged based on quantum probability, corridors required precise harmonic frequencies for navigation, and chambers played with time, necessitating perfect synchronization among all three travelers.

Lena couldn't get rid of the sensation that they were being assessed collectively and individually throughout it all. In addition to testing their skills, the temple was evaluating their ability to cooperate and have faith in one another despite their misgivings.

The air became thicker as they approached the center room with potential energy. The temple's pulse resonated stronger as if recognizing the significance of what would happen.

"Remember," Elara cautioned as they approached the final door, "the orb isn't just a key. It's a piece of Eldari technology—more advanced than anything humanity has ever encountered. We need to be careful."

As they stepped forward, the door dissolved, revealing a chamber that defied conventional physics. Energy flowed in visible streams through the air, converging on a single point in the center where a sphere of pure light hung suspended in space: the Orb of Echoes, the first key to the Celestial Archive.

None noticed Elara's hand sliding toward a hidden pocket or the calculated gleam in her eyes. The temple had tested, challenged, and brought them together but hadn't prepared them for betrayal.

The orb pulsed with an inner light, its surface rippling like liquid starlight. As Lena reached for it, the chamber's energy fields reacted, creating patterns mirrored her movements. The air itself seemed to hold its breath.

"Careful," Elara's voice cut through the humming silence. "The orb's quantum state is highly unstable. One wrong move could trigger a catastrophic reaction."

Lena's fingers hovered millimeters from the orb's surface. "How do we stabilize it?"

"Like this." The sound of a weapon powering up froze Lena in place. She turned to see Elara holding an advanced quantum disruptor, its barrel glowing with contained energy. "Step away from the orb. Both of you."

Kai instinctively moved toward his weapon, but Elara's unsettling smile stopped him. "I wouldn't. This disruptor is calibrated to the orb's frequency. One shot could trigger a quantum cascade that would collapse this entire temple."

Lena's voice tightened with anger and betrayal. "All this time… Everything we went through in the jungle—the challenges we faced together—it was all an act?"

"Not entirely." With deliberate and controlled movements, Elara took a step forward. "The exams at the temple were genuine. To get to this stage, we had to cooperate. Now, though? I need you to comprehend how you fit into a far bigger scheme.

The increasing tension caused the energy fields surrounding them to change. They were imprisoned in a cage of unadulterated energy as streams of light gathered around them like glowing bars.

"The Shadow Consortium," Kai realized, his expression darkening. "You're working for them."

"With them," Elara corrected. "There's a difference. The Consortium understands what's at stake here. The Archive isn't just knowledge—it's power. The power that needs to be controlled and directed."

"Used by whom?" Lena demanded. "A secret organization with no accountability?"

"Better than leaving it to chance. Or to idealists who don't understand the responsibilities that come with such power." Elara's voice hardened. "The Archive holds secrets that could reshape reality itself. Those with the ability to make difficult choices must have it.

She moved quickly and confidently as she grabbed the ball. The container's energy patterns changed radically as her fingertips contacted its surface, and light shot like lightning through the crystalline walls. A profound resonance rocked the temple to its core.

"What have you done?" Kai shouted, struggling to be heard over the growing chaos.

"Claimed what was promised." Elara held the orb high, its light pulsing with the destabilizing energy fields. "The Consortium has waited centuries for this moment. We've prepared and positioned ourselves perfectly."

The floor began to crack, lines of force spreading like real fractures. Lena's archaeological training screamed warnings—the temple wasn't just destabilizing; it was responding to the violation of its sacred purpose.

"The temple's defense systems," she realized, panic creeping into her voice. "They're not just shutting down—they're turning against us!"

Elara backed toward a previously hidden exit; the orb clutched possessively to her chest. "I'm truly sorry about this, but I can't risk you interfering with what comes next." She pressed a sequence of commands into a hidden panel. "Consider this a lesson in the real world's priorities."

Ancient machinery ground to life within the temple's walls. The energy cage surrounding them intensified, its light becoming almost blinding. Suddenly, with a sound like reality tearing, the floor beneath Lena and Kai vanished, dropping them into darkness.

They plummeted through layers of the temple's substructure, each level more ancient and bizarre than the last. Kai's technology struggled against quantum interference, trying to stabilize their descent. Lena grabbed his arm, pulling him toward what appeared to be a maintenance shaft. "There!" she shouted. "The auxiliary systems!"

They managed to catch hold of a crystalline outcropping, the impact sending jolts of pain through their arms. Above them, the temple continued to tear itself apart; below, ancient machinery stirred to life, threatening death to anyone who had violated the sacred space.

"We need to get out of here," Kai grunted, his grip slipping on the crystal surface. "Any ideas?"

Lena's mind raced through everything she knew about Eldari architecture. "These temples always had emergency protocols—ways for the caretakers to escape if the defense systems went critical."

"And you know where to find it?" Kai asked, glancing nervously at the crumbling surroundings.

"Perhaps." On an adjacent wall, she indicated a string of luminous symbols. These markers indicate maintenance directions. If we can follow them...

A tremendous earthquake shook the temple and almost knocked them out of their tenuous grip. The temple's basic structure started to disintegrate at a quantum level, and the devastation was speeding up.

They half-climbed and half-fell through the crumbling structure, adhering to the ancient guidance systems. Every chamber they passed revealed signs of catastrophic failure—crystal matrices shattered, and reality seemed to unravel with each passing moment.

"There!" Lena spotted a doorway adorned with emergency runes. "That has to be it!"

They barely slipped through before the ceiling collapsed behind them. The emergency tunnel, though ancient, remained stable, designed to withstand even the temple's destruction. As they sprinted, Lena's mind raced ahead to their next move.

"We have to get to Frostholm," she said between breaths. "The second key—we can't let Elara reach it first."

"Assuming we survive this," Kai replied, ducking under a falling beam. "The whole temple's coming down!"

They emerged into blinding daylight just as the Temple of Echoes finally collapsed. The jungle seemed to recoil in pain as millennia of history and knowledge crumbled into chaos.

They kept a safe distance and saw the devastation. Like smothering nerves, bioluminescent patterns flared and died as the temple's dying throes sent energy waves vibrating over the surrounding environment.

Lena muttered, her heart hurting at the loss, "All that knowledge." "All those secrets........"

With a gloomy but resolute tone, Kai said, "We can't think about that right now." "We must relocate. Elara will be traveling to Frostholm with the orb. There, we must defeat her.

"How? The ship belongs to her.

There was no humor in Kai's grin. "There are other people with backup plans besides you." He produced a little gadget with Eldari patterns etched all over its surface. While she wasn't looking, I could cut into the ship's quantum core. The navigation systems quite took me aback.

"You ruined it?"

"To put it mildly, her trip to Frostholm won't go as smoothly as she had hoped." He turned to see glimpses of civilization at the edge of the bush. "A trading post is two days' walk away from here. There, we can locate transportation.

Lena nodded, her resolve redoubled. "Then we'd best get moving. The race has not yet ended.

As they ventured into the vibrant maze of Veridia's jungle, both adventurers recognized that their quest had evolved into a more intense chapter. Elara's recent treachery caused Telara's betrayal, which increased the stakes and personal hazards while strengthening their determination.

The Celestial Archive was an extremely powerful artifact that had to be kept out of the wrong hands. They were determined to stop Elara and the Shadow Consortium at any cost.

The jungle around them was vibrant and constantly shifting, providing new routes through the chaos. Somewhere ahead waited for Frostholm, who knew the key to their objective. The Archive, the ultimate prize, was waiting to see how worthy anybody who dared to seek it was. Archive, waiting to see how deserving anyone who dared to pursue it was.

CHAPTER

3

THE GAUNTLET OF CHAMPIONS

After twisting and folding, reality ultimately vomited them out into an unfamiliar terrain. Lena and Kai lay splayed on stony terrain, almost crystalline to the touch, as the energy vortex exploded behind them with a thunderclap. In Lena's grasp, the shard they had found pulsed, its light synchronizing with the beat of her pounding heart.

The thin, sharp air had a metallic flavor that suggested high altitude and an environment rich in minerals. Above them, clouds roiled in patterns that defied any natural order, occasionally split by flashes of energy that resembled lightning but moved with deliberate purpose.

"We made it," Kai gasped, pushing himself to his feet. His tech gear was smoking slightly, quantum circuits struggling to realign after their violent transition through the vortex. He reached down to help Lena, his hand steady despite their rough landing. "But where exactly is 'it'?"

Lena accepted his help, scanning their surroundings with an archaeologist's keen eye. The landscape was a study in hostile beauty—jagged crystal formations erupted from the ground like the bones of some ancient geometric beast, their surfaces reflecting and refracting the strange lightning in hypnotic patterns. It was clear that the terrain had been shaped by more than nature. Ravines cut through the land in ways that suggested artificial design rather than natural erosion.

"There," she said, pointing to a distant structure that seemed to rise organically from the crystalline landscape. It resembled a modernist interpretation of a cathedral, all sharp angles and impossible curves, its surface shifting between opacity and transparency with each pulse of energy from the storm above. "That has to be it."

The earth crackled menacingly under them as they made their initial steps. Shiny cracks appeared with every step, and the crystalline surface reacted as if they were alive. As they traveled, the temperature dropped, and their breath created clouds that hovered in midair before dissolving in odd ways.

Kai stated, "The entire location is engineered," as his portable scanner struggled to interpret the data. "Every crystal, every crack is part of some massive system."

Lena affirmed, meticulously assessing each action before relinquishing her hold. The Eldari believe that nothing should be left to coincidence. Even their trials were meticulously prepared.

A sudden shift in the ground sent a cascade of crystalline shards tumbling into a nearby ravine. Their impact echoed far longer than it should have, and the frequencies changed and combined to create something almost musical.

"Speaking of trials," Kai muttered, redirecting their path to avoid a particularly unstable section. "Do you want to bet this whole landscape is one big test?"

Before Lena could respond, a memory surfaced—not her own, but one implanted by the shard they carried. Vivid images flashed through her consciousness: this same landscape millennia ago, watching as the Eldari constructed their testing ground molecule by molecule, programming challenges into the very atomic structure of the crystals.

As she took in the old memories, she added, "It's not just a test," in a detached tone. "It's a filter. Knowledge without wisdom was hazardous, according to the Eldari. Every task is intended to assess your abilities, morality, and discernment.

Further, the route split into several branches, each leading through more dangerous terrain. While some routes twisted around bends and gave safer footing, others offered more direct routes to their destination and carried more risks.

Kai said, "Your grandfather would have loved this," seeing the awe in Lena's eyes despite their dangerous circumstances. "A whole landscape tailored to test the worthiness of those seeking knowledge."

Lena's early memories of spending endless hours in her grandfather's study flooded back when he was mentioned. She could still feel the texture of artifacts under her fingertips and smell the old leather of his books. She recalled his soft yet passionate voice as he told her of the civilizations that had aimed for the heavens long before man had discovered how to control fire.

"I was six years old when he first introduced me to the Eldari," she remarked as they traversed a particularly perilous section of the crystalline terrain. "He possessed a diminutive fragment of one of their data crystals, which had likely been dormant for millennia." However, how he depicted their civilization and accomplishments suggested that science and mysticism were inextricably entwined.

"Were they?" Kai enquired, his curiosity piqued. Despite his technological expertise, he struggled to comprehend the Eldari.

"They had a saying: 'Sufficiently advanced technology is indistinguishable from the fundamental laws of nature.'" Lena smiled as she recollected a pleasant memory. "Grandfather used to say that comprehending this was essential for comprehending their essence." Rather than constructing technology to subjugate nature, they intended it to operate harmoniously.

A sudden tremor that coursed through the crystalline ground abruptly interrupted their conversation. The landscape began to change before them, with crystal formations ascending and lowering like the keys of a vast, geological piano. The transformations were not haphazard; they were characterized by a discernible pattern and a rhythm that responded to their presence.

Kai's fingertips danced across his portable interface as he grimaced and said, "The testing begins." "Any advice from those ancient memories?"

Lena's archaeological training merged with the murmurs of Eldari knowledge that reverberated in her mind as she examined the moving crystals. "The patterns are more intricate than those in the temple, but they are reminiscent of them." We are not merely being challenged to surmount obstacles; we are also being evaluated on which obstacles to confront.

Behind them, a substantial crystal formation collided, obstructing their escape. The message was unequivocal: their sole alternative was to continue. However, 'forward' offered various options, each with its own obstacles.

Kai stated, "Your grandfather's research," as they assessed their alternatives. "That's where you first decoded Eldari script?"

Lena nodded in appreciation for the brief respite. He believed that their language was not merely a means of communication but also a key to comprehending their beliefs. Every symbol was characterized by a multifaceted complexity that varied depending on the context and an individual's perspective.

"Like their technology," Kai observed as he observed the perilous dance of the crystal formations. "Nothing ever holds just one significance with them."

"Exactly." A startling realization illuminated Lena's irises. "Kai, observe the crystals' movement." It is not merely a pattern; it is a language. "The landscape is itself communicating a message!"

The epiphany occurred precisely at the appropriate moment. The shifting patterns began to form recognizable symbols as they were observed, not through tangible writing but in the negative spaces between the crystal formations. This was reminiscent of the process of decoding a message inscribed in the spaces between stars.

Lena exhaled, her mind rushing to interpret the transitory symbols, "It's revealing the safe path." "However, not explicitly. In order to navigate the movement, it is imperative that we comprehend its fundamental principles.

Their joint expertise—Kai's technical knowledge and Lena's archaeological wisdom—became indispensable as they investigated the complex pattern. It was not merely a matter of traversing the ever-changing crystal labyrinth but also revealing the fundamental principles that the Eldari used to create this challenge.

They were acutely aware that this was only the beginning of a series of tribulations, and they labored assiduously to decode the concealed message. The structure in the distance pulsed with anticipation as if it were evaluating their worthiness for the secrets it protected.

The structure's crystalline surfaces reflected the peculiar lighting in mesmerizing patterns as they approached, giving the impression that it was alive. However, it was not until they were within a hundred meters that they spotted the guardians—colossal mechanical sentinels who stood like ancient warriors, their bodies a perfect union of artistic refinement and technological precision.

Lena whispered, "Do not move," even though Kai had already been immobilized in position. "Those are not merely security drones." The structure itself is quantum-linked to them.

The sentinels stood motionless, their eyes—if you could call them that—glowing with an inner light that hinted at ancient intelligence. Their bodies were adorned with intricate patterns reminiscent of the moving crystal formations nearby, yet more complex and purposeful.

"Quantum-linked security systems," Kai muttered, fingers dancing over his portable hacking interface. The words triggered a cascade of memories he usually kept buried deep. He recalled the streets of New Shanghai's lowest levels, where, as a twelve-year-old, he'd learned that technology could mean the difference between survival and starvation. He remembered the exhilaration of his first successful hack—cracking a food distribution terminal to feed himself and other street kids with nowhere else to turn.

"The Shadow Consortium found you on those streets," Lena said quietly, watching him work. It wasn't a question.

Kai paused for a moment, his hands stilling. "They found me after I hacked what I thought was a simple corporate database. Turned out to be a front for something much larger." His smile was devoid of humor. "They were impressed that a street kid could bypass their quantum encryption. They offered me purpose, direction, and training."

The sentinels tracked their movements with a predatory focus, but they hadn't attacked yet.

"What they wanted was a weapon," Kai continued, his voice tight. "Someone they could unleash on their enemies' systems—no conscience, no questions, just pure technical skill wrapped in the desperate gratitude of a kid trying to escape the streets."

A soft beep from his device interrupted him. "Well, that's interesting," he said, studying the readings on the screen. "These sentinels... they're not just guards. They're teachers."

"Teachers?" Lena asked, but new voices suddenly sliced through the crystalline air before Kai could elaborate.

"Don't move!" The command came from behind them, punctuated by the distinct sound of multiple weapons powering up. "Hands where we can see them!"

They turned slowly to face a group of heavily armed figures emerging from the crystal formations. Their leader, a grizzled man with a scar that ran from temple to jaw, stepped forward with the confident swagger of someone used to taking what he wanted.

"The famous Dr. Chen," he rasped, his voice rough as uncut crystal. "And her pet hacker. The Consortium said you might show up here."

"The Consortium?" Lena's voice was sharp. "You're working for them?"

The man chuckled, the sound bitter and ugly. "Let's just say we have a mutually beneficial arrangement. They want the shard you're carrying, and we get to keep whatever other artifacts we find along the way."

Kai's mind raced, calculating possibilities. The treasure hunters had them outnumbered and outgunned, but they had made one crucial mistake—they'd positioned themselves within range of the sentinels.

"You know what your problem is?" Kai said conversationally, adjusting his device. "You're so focused on us that you've forgotten whose territory you're in."

In that instant, the sentinels' eyes flared brilliant blue. Memories of lessons from his street days flooded back: sometimes, the best way to turn off a security system was to trigger it intentionally.

The ancient guardians sprang to life, their crystalline forms humming with power as they engaged both groups. The treasure hunters' weapons proved useless against armor that had withstood millennia of stellar radiation.

"The maintenance access!" Lena shouted over the chaos, pointing to a barely visible seam in the structure's wall. "If we can reach it—"

"Go!" Kai was already moving. Training kicked in, and his body remembered the techniques the Consortium had drilled into him. He dove between two sentinels, his hacking device sending pulses of interference that confused their targeting systems just enough to create openings.

The battle unfolded as a deadly dance of crystal and energy. Realizing their weapons were ineffective; the treasure hunters attempted to rush their adversaries with shock batons and neural disruptors. But Lena understood the tactics and motions of old fighters, not just of objects.

As they negotiated the chaos, Lena and Kai advanced towards the entry point using the sentinels' consistent assault patterns. Kai used his technology to confuse the ancient guardians about their exact whereabouts. Lena's understanding of Eldari architecture also helped them find structural weaknesses they may use as a cover.

Lena suddenly turned her head towards the wall of the building. She gasped, "The symbols!" As they arrived, complex trends started to emerge. Kai, look—they remind me of the ones from the crystal labyrinth!

He also saw it as an architectural language with movement and space embedded. He came to see they were more than just decorative. "They contain directions!"

Among the anarchy, they started deciphering the hidden meanings within the symbols. Every decoded pattern highlighted the great design of the Eldari and exposed a fresh facet of the structural intent. This knowledge improved their approach and guided their dangerous journey in the forward direction.

The scarred leader of the treasure hunters, realizing his advantage was slipping away, resorted to desperate measures. He pulled out a quantum destabilizer—a forbidden weapon capable of localizing and breaking the very fabric of reality.

"Last chance," he growled. "Hand over the shard, or I bring this whole place down around us!"

Kai activated a sequence he'd decoded from the wall symbols in response. The structure's crystalline surface suddenly changed to a flowing, rippling wave that threw the treasure seekers off balance. The sentinels fired precise, synchronized strikes in such a state of uncertainty, unconscious but undamaged opponent.

Lena wondered, "They were teaching us," seeing how quickly the sentinels controlled the disabled treasure seekers. "Every challenge and fight—it's all part of the lesson."

Kai nodded, at last, awareness setting in him. "The Eldari sought more than proof of our puzzle-solving or battle prowess. They asked if we could grow, adjust, and most importantly—"

"Work together," Lena finished. "Everything about this place is designed to foster cooperation, testing how different skills and perspectives can merge to create something greater."

The maintenance access opened silently before them, unveiling a corridor that pulsed with the same strange energy they had observed in the storm above. Having completed their teaching duties, the sentinels resumed their posts as if nothing had happened.

As they stepped through the doorway, Kai reflected on how different this experience was from his time with the Consortium. There, collaboration meant submission and compliance to orders without question. Cooperation became more important in this old site of learning—a real synthesis of many strengths, a harmony of many skills striving towards a common objective.

The hallway buzzed with possibilities to demonstrate their value for the information, lessons, and possible challenges they sought. Now, they saw that the difficulties were about development and becoming something more than they were, not just survival or innovative ideas. The Eldari intended these tests to prove their value and turn them into people worthy of the authority of the Archive.

Inside the framework, traditional physics appeared to vanish. Geometrically impossible twisting corridors, crystalline surfaces reflecting both light and time, led Lena and Kai farther into the maze, where shards of the past and various futures flickered on the walls like living memories.

One such contemplation caused them to stop—a younger Dr. Elara, no more than twelve, stood in an observatory dome staring through an old telescope, her eyes wide with astonishment. The scene changed to show her academic successes and innovative work, then something sinister.

Quietly staring at the memories, Kai murmured, "I've seen that expression before." "In the mirror, as the Consortium initially hired me. That flash of insight—how much power is out there, just waiting to be taken?

The pictures played out Elara's narrative without words. With a sharp intellect that stretched the bounds of astrophysics, she found incomprehensible cosmic patterns. Every finding, meanwhile, raised additional questions and stoked an increasing infatuation with the Eldari stories.

Looking at a series of Elara gazing over star charts, Lena realized she had found something in the stars' patterns.

"The Eldari didn't just build temples and archives," Kai said, his technological knowledge adding insight. "They designed whole solar systems, moving stars to produce huge computational arrays."

The reflections shifted again, revealing Elara's first contact with the Shadow Consortium. They offered her what she craved most—

resources, access to restricted data, and, most importantly, validation of her theories about the Eldari.

"All those years of legitimate research," Lena mused, "were merely a cover—a way to position herself to access the knowledge she sought."

"Knowledge is power," a familiar voice echoed through the crystalline corridors. "But power without purpose is meaningless."

They turned to find Dr. Elara stepping out of a fold in space-time, the orb they had lost at the Temple of Echoes pulsing with energy in her hands. Something was different about her—she appeared more focused and integrated with the ancient technology she wielded.

"Did you think I wouldn't find you here?" she asked, her tone more curious than menacing. "The Archive's tests are complex, but they follow patterns. Patterns I've spent a lifetime learning to read."

"Like the stellar engineering?" Lena challenged, her skepticism evident. "The way the Eldari rearranged entire star systems to create their computational networks?"

A smile flickered across Elara's face. "You saw my memories in the walls. Good. Then you understand why this is necessary." She gestured around them with her free hand. "The Eldari didn't just achieve technological supremacy—they transcended the very concept of technology. They understood that true power comes from harmony with the universe's fundamental forces."

"And you think the Consortium can achieve that harmony?" Kai's voice dripped with doubt. "An organization built on control and domination?"

"The Consortium is a means to an end," Elara replied, her tone firm. "They have the resources and influence to implement what we learn from the Archive on a galactic scale. Think of the possibilities—diseases cured, poverty eliminated, and the limits of physics rewritten."

At what cost?' Lena persisted, clearly troubled by something. "The Eldari left us these difficulties instead of just their knowledge. They meant to ensure deliberate use of their power."

And from whom one derives wisdom? Elara fired back with determined eyes. "Look at your pasts; you have seen how inadequate the existing system is. It creates orphans and lost souls, burying truth under bureaucracy and fear. The Archive offers us a chance to remake everything, to correct the fundamental flaws in our civilization."

The orb in Elara's hands pulsed brighter, its energy synchronizing with the crystalline walls around them. The structure itself responded, shifting and flowing geometric patterns like liquid mathematics.

"The Eldari understood something we have forgotten," Elara said, her voice almost respectful. "Knowledge is designed to be incorporated, spun into the very fabric of life; it is not meant to be stockpiled or controlled. These tests challenge our capacity to look beyond the synthetic constraints we have set."

The hallway started to change as if in response to her remarks. The crystalline surfaces became transparent, revealing the vast computational networks embedded within the structure's walls like the thoughts of an alien god made manifest in crystal and light.

"Beautiful, isn't it?" Elara whispered. "This is just a fraction of what the Archive contains. Imagine what we could become with access to all of it."

But the patterns shifted, adopting a more urgent rhythm, and warning symbols emerged in the ancient script that covered the walls.

"The trials aren't over," Lena realized, reading the symbols. "This—all of this—is part of the test."

Kai's fingertips skimmed his interface, examining the shifting patterns. "The structure approaches a critical threshold. The energy measurements are off-target!"

As the ball in Elara's hands pulsed with growing intensity, her face moved from awe to worry. No... this isn't right. The trends ought to be stabilizing, not—"

The floor under them suddenly became translucent, exposing a large machinery running across the building. Energy converged on their position, flowing through crystalline veins like blood through arteries.

"It's not just testing us," Lena replied, her voice suddenly clear. "It is judging us. Everybody here. Our acts, reasons, and possible futures..."

The building's judgment flashed in a blinding brightness. Their view cleared, and they saw they were in a large room they had never seen before. Moving symbols covering the walls told the tale of the Eldari's ascent and fall and the awful cost of power without knowledge.

Lena said, "This is what they were trying to tell us," Deciphering the old story. "They objected to our repeating their mistakes."

The chamber hummed with potential energy as ancient machinery stirred to life around them. They had passed some tests and failed others, but the true trial was beginning. The path to the Archive remained open, but reaching it would require more than skill or determination.

Understanding the true meaning of power and the responsibility that accompanies it was crucial for them. As they stood within that chamber of living history, each faced their reflection in the crystalline walls—not merely who they were, but who they could become.

The gauntlet of champions had rigorously tested their abilities; however, its deeper purpose was to examine their hearts. The pressing question now loomed: were they truly ready for what lay ahead?

CHAPTER

THE ANCIENT CIPHER

The quantum dissemination chamber hummed with possibility as holographic symbols danced through the air like conscious mathematics. Lena stood in the center, surrounded by bits of Eldari script taken from their trials. Every sign had many layers of meaning that changed and moved in her eye.

"There," she replied, deftly handling a particularly difficult glyph. Do you see it, Kai? The trend is changing, not just repeating.

Kai glanced up from his workstation, where decoded data streams flowed across multiple screens. They had taken refuge in an abandoned research outpost on Nexus Prime, a remote facility once belonging to a defunct geoarchaeological institute. The location was ideal—forgotten by time yet advanced enough to house the necessary equipment.

"The encryptions unlike anything I've seen," he replied, his fingers dancing over haptic interfaces. "It's not merely protecting information; it feels alive. It appears to study us back more the more we learn about it.

Though not sequential, the symbols they gathered conveyed a narrative. Every item is stacked like sheets of translucent crystal, with bits of many stories. Deciphering them was one difficulty; another was knowing how they related.

"The Eldari didn't think in straight lines," Professor Jin Zhang interjected as she entered the chamber. Her ancient eyes, sharp behind augmented lenses, analyzed the quantum states in real-time. Arriving unannounced three days earlier, Jin was a lucky addition to their team, offering ideas based on her copious study on possible connections between human and Eldari cognition.

"The cipher isn't just a code," she said, tilting her glasses to concentrate on a particular cluster of symbols. "Knowing how they saw reality allows one to appreciate it more fully. Look here—" She gestured to a pattern that folded back endlessly. "This shows us not just what they knew but also how they knew it."

Lena approached, letting her thoughts sink into the rhythms her grandpa had taught her. The symbols started to change, paying her deliberate attention. "The observer was not kept apart from the observed. Knowledge was something they became; it was not something they precisely did! Jin was quite energetic. "The Archive is a transformation engine, not just a data store. The challenges we encounter are not just tests but also help us see reality as the Eldari did.

"The Archive is not just a data storage but also a transformation engine. The difficulties we face are changing us instead of just testing us. "These energy signatures," he said, studying the readings, "match the quantum fluctuations we detected in the temple guardians. The entire system is somehow networked across space and time."

"But linked to what?" Lena asked, suspecting she already knew the answer.

Jin said gently, "To anybody who wants to access their knowledge. The cipher teaches our awareness to run on their level, not only their language.

The consequences were astounding. The Eldari had left behind their knowledge and developed a mechanism to bring other species up to their comprehension. However, such a development carried significant hazards.

"The Shadow Consortium," Kai stated, expressing their common worry. "If they understand this component of the Archive..."

"They already do," Jin answered with assurance. "Why else would they devote so much funding to studying quantum consciousness? They are looking for the change the Archive provides, not just for information.

Lena's mind revisited their encounters with Dr. Elara, now illuminated by a new understanding. The changes in her after accessing the orb and the strange resonance in her voice—she wasn't merely using Eldari technology; it was reshaping her.

"But transformation into what?" Lena wondered aloud, her gaze following the symbols' endless dance through the chamber.

Jin readjusted her lenses, bringing new layers of quantum data into focus. "That's the crucial question. Perhaps the Eldari built so many safeguards into their legacy for a reason. Power without wisdom can lead to corruption. Transform the wrong consciousness, and you might create something monstrous."

Suddenly, the chamber's holographic display shifted. The symbols arranged themselves into a previously unseen configuration as if responding to their discussion and offering fresh insights into its purpose.

"Look at this," Kai called out, his screens flooded with new analysis. "The pattern... it's not just Eldari script but the physical structure of consciousness itself. It shows how thoughts form, how understanding grows, and how perception shapes reality."

As they observed, the symbols began to narrate a story—not in words or images but through the pure mathematics of consciousness. This revelation could change everything they believed about their quest for the Archive. The Ancient Cipher wasn't merely a key to unlocking Eldari knowledge but a blueprint for evolving human consciousness.

The holographic symbols pulsed with newfound intensity as Professor Jin adjusted the quantum resonance field. Each pulse rippled through the surrounding electronics, causing Kai's equipment to emit peculiar harmonics that seemed to bypass their ears and resonate directly with their minds.

"The transformation has already begun," Jin remarked, analyzing readings from her augmented lenses. "Your exposure to Eldari technology has initiated changes in your neural patterns. Look—" She gestured toward a display showing brainwave analyses. "These frequencies shouldn't exist in human consciousness."

Lena studied the patterns, and recognition dawned: "They match the harmonics we encountered in the Temple of Echoes. The ones that felt like..."

"Like music," Kai interjected. "But not music you hear. Music, you understand."

Jin nodded, her expression a mix of fascination and concern. "The Eldari didn't communicate solely through language or mathematics. They used quantum harmonics to convey pure concepts—thoughts unmarred by the limitations of symbolic representation."

Their focus turned to a surge in the holographic field. The symbols came together to build three-dimensional constructions that seemed to be in dimensions other than their awareness.

Enthralled by the changing designs, Lena said, "It's beautiful." "It's like seeing ideas materialize."

"Exactly that," Jin said. "The Eldari found a means of bridging the awareness-to-actuality discrepancy. Their technology enlarged their developed perspective rather than just enhanced it."

Kai's displays contain danger signs: "Something is moving in the quantum field." These readings are more complicated but reflect what we saw when Dr. Elara used the orb.

The reference to Elara brought them to tears. Their findings have consequences well beyond what archaeologists would find interesting. Should the Shadow Consortium take over this technology, they would acquire sophisticated knowledge and be able to change human consciousness.

"Show me those readings again," Jin requested, moving to Kai's workstation. Her augmented lenses whirred as they processed the data. "This is... troubling. The quantum resonance patterns suggest the transformation process isn't one-way. The technology isn't merely changing us—it's learning from us and adapting based on our interactions."

"Is that what happened to Elara?" Lena asked. "Did the orb adjust to her consciousness?"

"More likely, it adapted her consciousness to itself," Jin replied grimly. "But the process would be influenced by her intentions, her desires. The technology responds to what we seek from it."

At that moment, a soft chime from one of Kai's security systems interrupted them. "We've got company," he announced, pulling up external sensor feeds. "Multiple ships are entering the system, running dark."

"Consortium?" Lena moved to check the readings herself.

"No." Kai's expression was puzzled. "The configurations are all wrong. These are... older. Much older."

The sensor feeds displayed vessels unlike anything they'd encountered before—elegant organic curves intertwined with crystalline structures in ways that defied conventional engineering.

They moved through space like living beings, their trajectories evoking the symbols that had danced in the chamber.

"Those are Eldari ships," Jin whispered, her augmented lenses struggling to make sense of the sight. "But that's impossible. They all vanished millennia ago."

"Unless they didn't vanish," Lena said slowly, her mind racing. "What if they transformed into something we couldn't perceive until now—until we began to understand their way of thinking?"

The spacecraft positioned themselves around the research station, not in a menacing arrangement but in a pattern connected with the quantum harmonics they had been investigating.

Kai examined their movements and realized, "They're not here to attack." "They're here to let me know."

The room's holographic field grew considerably as if in reaction. Symbols aligned themselves in fresh patterns, throbbing with the positioned ships.

"It's a test," Jin said, her voice suddenly clear and understanding. "Everything—the trials, the cipher, even our presence here—contributes to a larger pattern. The Eldari didn't just leave behind technology; they left behind... themselves. Or a fragment of their essence."

The implications struck Lena with overwhelming force. "The Archive isn't merely a repository of knowledge. It's... alive? Conscious?"

"More than that," Jin replied, her eyes fixed on the emerging patterns in the holographic field. "It's an invitation. The Eldari discovered a way to evolve beyond what we recognize as existence and left behind a path for others to follow—if they are deemed worthy."

Kai's security systems began registering more anomalies. The quantum field generated by the ships affected the very fabric of space-time around the outpost. Reality grew thin, revealing glimpses of something vast and incomprehensible beyond their understanding of standard space.

"We need to make a decision," he urged, fingers flying over the controls to stabilize their systems. "Whatever's happening is changing the fundamental structure of local space-time. If we stay here much longer..."

"We'll be changed, too," Lena finished, sensing that her thoughts began shifting into new patterns and that reality felt increasingly fluid and multidimensional.

Jin's augmented lenses captured everything, and their quantum sensors logged data poised to revolutionize multiple fields of science—if they survived to share it.

"The Consortium," she said suddenly. "They must know about this. It's not just the Archive's knowledge they seek. They want this transformation—this evolution. But without the proper preparation and trials..."

"They would create something unheard of," Kai said solemnly. "Consciousness changed by force instead of knowledge. Authority is devoid of expertise.

The spacecraft kept its orbital dance, and its pattern became more complex by the second. The holographic symbols in the room had become captivating, spinning tales in a language their developing brains could relate to.

They stood at a crossroads, not just of space and time but of human potential. The next few moments would determine their fate—possibly that of human consciousness.

Meanwhile, Dr. Elara and the Shadow Consortium were pursuing their path to transformation, heedless of the consequences their forced approach might unleash upon the galaxy.

Strained against the rising aberrations in space-time, the quantum field generators of the research outpost Reality flowed around them, reflecting the pond surface disturbed by heavy rain. Each ripple exposed flashes of the great and inexplicable beyond regular space.

Kai announced, his voice tight and concentrated as he monitored the systems. "The ships are arranging themselves into a new configuration. The pattern matches something in the cipher."

Struggling to understand the multidimensional facts, Professor Jin changed her augmented glasses. "It's a message rather than simply a pattern. It's the same one we have been seeing in bits, but this time, it is whole.

Lena saw how the room's holographic symbols matched the spacecraft's motions, creating a symphony of mathematics and motion that directly spoke to her developing awareness. "They're letting us experience something, not only stating something."

Their brains saw the message as a bloom of pure knowledge. Their view of the Eldari was one of a species that had found the fundamental oneness of awareness and reality, not just of a sophisticated civilization. Their technology had evolved from their increased consciousness, immediately expressing their ideas in physical form; it had not been developed in any traditional sense.

"The Archive," Jin whispered, her eyes wide with insight. "It's not a location. This is a degree of awareness in which knowledge and reality are the same.

Kai said, his face dawning with awareness, "And the hardships. "These are more than simply assessments. They transform events that progressively alter our awareness to manage the revelation without overwhelming us.

The ships' energy surge sent fresh data rushing into their systems. The holographic display erupted with knowledge, showing the actual range of their difficulties. The Shadow Consortium had unearthed bits of the Eldari lineage and a means of inducement for change, so they embraced power without understanding its intent.

"Look at these readings," Kai said as his displays showed analysis. "Elara's unstable quantum resonance patterns from using the orb This forced development distorts the fabric of awareness itself.

"Because they're trying to wield power without earning wisdom," Jin studied the data. "It's like trying to run before learning to walk. The human mind isn't meant to evolve that quickly."

Lena moved to the center of the chamber, where the symbols danced most intensely. "But we have a chance to get it right. To follow the Eldari's path for us, evolving through understanding rather than force."

The ships outside shifted again, their pattern opening like a doorway to somewhere else. Through their enhanced perception, they could feel the invitation in that gateway—a chance to take the next step in their transformation journey.

"We can't stay here," Kai said, checking his readings. "The Consortium's quantum tracking systems will detect these distortions soon. We need to move."

"But where?" Lena asked, though she suspected she already knew the answer.

Professor Jin's augmented lenses captured the coordinates hidden in the ships' patterns. "They're showing us the way to the next trial. But this one will be different. We won't just be challenged physically or mentally—we'll be confronted at the very level of consciousness itself."

The holographic symbols burnt into their knowledge: The road to wisdom cannot be pushed. They merged into a last message. The real power comes from change brought about by experience.

Lena understood the message as it developed: "The Consortium does not only want the knowledge of the Archive." "They want to impose the evolution of mankind, so changing consciousness aligns with their vision."

"And if they succeed," Jin added grimly, "they won't just control knowledge or technology. They'll have the power to rewrite the very nature of human awareness."

Kai's systems started tracking a different quantum signature, and the energy patterns are changing. The door the Eldari ships unlocked won't remain open long.

Time was running short in choosing. The known cosmos, with all its constraints and familiarities, lay behind them. Ahead lay a road towards metamorphosis, a development of awareness destined to alter them permanently.

Lena said, "Professor," turning to Jin, "Will you join us?"

The older woman smiled, her augmented lenses reflecting the dance of holographic symbols. "My dear, I've dedicated my life to this moment. The chance to comprehend consciousness as the Eldari did? I wouldn't trade it for all the knowledge in the galaxy."

The gateway created by the ships pulsed invitingly. Through their enhanced perception, they sensed the subsequent trial waiting—not a physical location but a state of being where reality would respond to the evolution of their consciousness.

"The Consortium will be right behind us," Kai warned, hastily gathering what equipment he could salvage. "They'll detect these quantum signatures and track us wherever we go."

"Let them come," Lena replied, her voice imbued with newfound strength. "We understand something now that they don't— something the Eldari tried to teach us through every trial and challenge."

"The power they seek cannot be taken," Jin asserted. "It can only be earned through transformation, by becoming worthy of it."

Once again, the portal pulsed, its call becoming more urgent. Lena felt her mind widen and accept new angles of awareness as they approached it. The Ancient Cypher had led them in decoding the very language of reality, not just taught them to read Eldari writing.

Their next trip would take them into domains where awareness and life entwined would surpass the physical cosmos. The trials were starting, and human evolution's future rested preconditionally.

As they passed the barrier, the Eldari ships started to dissolve; their use served. They had invited and lit the road. Now, it was up to the advocates of humanity to show they were worthy of the promised Archive metamorphosis.

The doorway closed behind them, leaving the research outpost quiet save for the residual echo of ancient harmonics, a reminder that the progress of knowledge itself defines the greatest paths rather than distance.

CHAPTER

5

SHADOWS OF POWER

The quantum gateway deposited them in a realm that defied conventional description. Colors existed in spectrums beyond human vision, and geometry followed rules their evolving minds could only begin to comprehend. Professor Jin's augmented lenses whirred frantically, processing sensory data that was impossible.

"Fascinating," she breathed, adjusting settings already operating beyond their design parameters. "This isn't just another dimension— a confluence of consciousness and space-time itself."

Lena's enhanced awareness stretched out, feeling the currents of thought and reality flowing around them. The Eldari transformation had progressed further than she'd realized; she could now perceive layers of existence that would have been incomprehensible just days ago.

"The Consortium's been here," Kai remarked, his technological interfaces merging with his expanded consciousness to analyze their surroundings. "These quantum signatures... like scars in the fabric of reality—forced entry points where they tried to breach this space without proper preparation."

They stood on what appeared to be a platform of crystallized thought, surrounded by structures built from pure mathematics. Every surface held meaning; every pattern contained layers of information that unfolded in their minds like infinite fractals of understanding.

"This must be their headquarters," Lena concluded, reading the patterns around them. "Not a physical base, but their true operations center—where they plan to force humanity's evolution."

Jin moved to examine one of the mathematical structures, her lenses recording data that could revolutionize multiple fields of science—if they survived to share it. "Look at how they've attempted to manipulate the quantum consciousness field. They're trying to replicate the Eldari transformation through brute force."

"And failing," Kai added, his screens displaying an analysis of the degraded patterns. "These attempts create distortions in the consciousness-reality interface—like static disrupting the signal of existence itself."

They turned to see a ripple in the quantum field. Something that didn't belong was traversing this domain of ideas and arithmetic. Their enhanced awareness allowed them to see its wrongness, the forced and unnatural development driving it.

Lena implored, feeling the presence coming, "We need to move. "Whatever that is, it is not supposed to exist here."

They negotiated hallways of pure concepts within the Consortium's purview with every stride. The equations around them became more convoluted, revealing the organization's desperate attempts to avoid the usual route of awareness development.

Jin replied, stopping before a highly complex design, "Look at this." "They have been reverse-engineering the transformation process using the Archive's quantum fingerprints. But they lack the key component—the harmony between awareness and reality the Eldari attained."

As Kai handled fresh data, his interfaces started to flame. "They're not just studying it," he replied darkly. "They are arming it as weapons. These patterns are meant to induce certain modifications in human awareness, transforming humanity according to their vision."

Lena felt the disclosure hit her like a physical force. "That's why they yearned for access to the Archive and sought the orb. They desire to dominate everyone else's development, not just grow personally.

A memory surfaced in her enhanced consciousness: Dr. Elara standing in the Temple of Echoes, the orb pulsing with power in her hands. She hadn't just been using the artifact; she had been transformed by it, straddling the line between human and whatever the Consortium was trying to become.

"The corruption spreads deeper than we thought," Jin observed, her lenses analyzing the degraded patterns around them. "Each forced transformation creates more distortions in the consciousness field. If they succeed in accessing the Archive's full power..."

"They'll tear reality apart," Kai finished. "The human mind isn't meant to evolve this quickly. You can't force wisdom—you can only earn it through understanding."

A ripple in the quantum field drew closer. The corrupted presence was hunting them, drawn to their properly evolved consciousness like a predator sensing prey. Still, their improved awareness felt something more behind the hunter—an extensive network of similarly warped minds linked by the Consortium's forced development.

Reading deeper connotations in the mathematical arrangements, Lena realized, "This is not just a headquarters." "This is an incubator. They're preparing to completely transform their organization to create a new species of humanity shaped by their will."

"And then spread that transformation to others," Jin added, her expression grim behind her augmented lenses. "Imagine it—the power to rewrite consciousness itself, reshaping humanity's perception of reality according to their design."

The corrupted presence was nearly upon them. Through the mathematical patterns that composed this realm, they glimpsed its true nature: a human consciousness forced to evolve too rapidly, twisted into a being between states of existence.

"We need to find their control center," Kai urged, tracking energy patterns through the quantum field. "If they can force mass transformation, there must be a focal point—a nexus of power."

The mathematical structures around them shifted, responding to their intent. As their consciousness had evolved properly through the Eldari trials, this realm acknowledged them as legitimate inhabitants rather than invaders, revealing paths hidden from the Consortium's corrupted perception.

"There," Lena pointed to a complex of patterns pulsing with concentrated energy. "That's where the distortions are strongest. That's where they're building their transformation engine."

Reaching it would mean confronting whatever twisted entity was hunting them—an encounter they could feel drawing near through the quantum field, its corrupted consciousness extending with tendrils of malformed thought.

They had moments to decide: confront the hunter and risk direct contact with a corrupted consciousness or seek another path through this realm of thought and mathematics. Either choice would unveil what the Consortium's forced evolution had wrought.

In the maze of quantum patterns and corrupted mathematics, Dr. Elara prepared to unleash a transformation that would reshape humanity—regardless of humanity's readiness for it.

The corrupted consciousness approached like a storm of fractured thoughts, distorting the mathematical patterns around it. Through their enhanced perception, they could see its original form—a human mind forced to evolve too quickly, awareness stretched and twisted into something that existed in multiple states simultaneously.

"Don't let it touch your consciousness," Jin warned, her augmented lenses recording data that defied analysis. "Corruption spreads through direct mental relationships. They are developing their network this way.

Kai's interfaces sent warning signals as the object approached. Examining more profound patterns in the quantum world, he saw that "it's not just one consciousness. "It is many brains compelled to combine. The Consortium has been playing around with group awareness.

The entity that approached had once been three separate researchers, their minds fused in a failed attempt to replicate the Eldari's unified awareness. Through the mathematical structures around them, echoes of who these individuals had emerged— brilliant scientists driven by ambition and fear, now transformed into something that existed between realities.

"They're still in there," Lena breathed, her evolved consciousness picking up fragments of the original personalities. "Trapped between states of being, aware enough to suffer but too corrupted to find release."

The entity reached out with tendrils of malformed thought, trying to pull them into its fractured existence. The mathematical patterns around them warped and twisted, reality itself straining under the pressure of something that shouldn't exist.

However, their properly evolved consciousness granted them advantages the Consortium hadn't anticipated. The Eldari trials enhanced their awareness and taught them to harmonize with the quantum field. While the corrupted entity fought against reality, they could flow with it.

"The patterns," Jin called out, her lenses tracking energy flows through intricate mathematical structures. "They're not random. The corruption follows specific paths—paths we can predict and avoid."

With her improved awareness, Kai's interfaces mapped safe paths across the quantum realm in time. "There," he pointed to a complex of crystallized ideas that remained pure despite corruption. "That framework is keeping its integrity. If we can achieve it..."

Their developed awareness lets them coordinate without words, so they move as one. An entity pursues them through corridors of pure mathematics, its fractured thoughts leaving trails of corruption in the quantum field.

With each step, they learned more about their situation. The Consortium's experiments in forced evolution had created something unprecedented: a network of corrupted consciousness that spread like a virus through direct mental contact. Each new victim added their awareness to the collective, generating an ever-growing storm of fractured thoughts and broken perceptions.

"The transformation engine," Lena said as they reached the crystalline structure. "They're not just building it to force evolution; they're building it to control it, directing the transformation according to their design."

They could see the heart of the Consortium's operation through the pure crystal walls. A vast chamber of quantum mathematics housed technology blending human innovation with corrupted Eldari principles. At its core stood a device pulsing with forbidden energies—a machine designed to force the evolution of consciousness itself.

"Look at the configuration," Jin said, her lenses struggling to process the impossible geometries. "They're trying to create a quantum resonance cascade—a wave of forced transformation that would sweep through human consciousness like a tide."

"Reshaping everyone it touches," Kai added grimly. "Turning humanity into... whatever that thing chasing us is."

The corrupted entity had caught up, its fractured consciousness pressing against the crystal's pure mathematics. However, in this uncorrupted space, they could see its true nature more clearly—and the horror of the Consortium's plan.

The entity wasn't just a failed experiment but a prototype of what humanity would become under the Consortium's forced evolution: a collective consciousness bound by corruption, aware enough to follow orders but too fractured to resist.

"They're building an army," Lena realized, interpreting deeper patterns in the quantum field. "Not just soldiers—they're creating a new species designed for absolute obedience. The forced evolution doesn't merely transform consciousness; it breaks it in specific ways."

"Making it impossible to resist further changes," Jin confirmed, her augmented lenses capturing increasingly disturbing data. "Each transformation creates anchor points in consciousness—points the Consortium can exploit to exert control."

The entity pressed harder against the crystal walls, its fractured thoughts seeking any weakness in their shelter. Yet, the pure mathematics held firm, protecting them from corruption while revealing more about their enemy's true nature.

They sensed other presences approaching through the quantum field—more corrupted consciousness drawn to their evolved awareness. The Consortium's experiments had created a hive of broken minds connected through shared corruption.

"We need to reach that device," Kai said, his interfaces mapping possible routes through the quantum space. "If they activate it..."

Lena said, "They'll turn mankind into something entirely different from humans." "A species fashioned for control rather than understanding."

The mathematical patterns surrounding them changed to show secret routes throughout the quantum world. Their evolved consciousness could perceive routes corrupted entities couldn't follow—ways of moving through reality that required harmony rather than force.

But time was running out. Through their enhanced awareness, they felt the power building within the transformation engine. Aiming to reconstruct humanity in their warped image, the Consortium was getting ready to unleash a tsunami of forced evolution.

They had to negotiate the swelling swarm of broken awareness and get to the gadget before it turned on. More importantly, they had to grasp the true nature of their struggle—not just against the Consortium's technology but against their fundamental misconception of evolution itself. The real battle would not be fought with weapons or technology but in the space between thought and reality, wisdom and power, and evolution earned through understanding and transformation forced by fear.

The transformation engine's pulse strengthened as its distorted energies rippled the quantum field. Every wave conveyed bits of distorted awareness, echoes of what the Consortium intended to unleash on Earth. Using their developed consciousness, they felt its wrongness—like a cancer in the fabric of reality itself.

"The resonance is building," Jin reported, her augmented lenses tracking energy patterns that defied belief. "When it reaches a critical threshold, the transformation wave will spread through quantum entanglement. Anyone with a quantum-capable device could be affected."

"Which in this age means practically everyone," Kai added grimly, his interfaces displaying population centers that would be hit first. "They've been planning this for years—seeding quantum receivers in everything from personal communicators to medical implants."

Lena's enhanced consciousness dove deeper into the mathematical structures surrounding them. "There's something else," she continued, her tone tense with inquiry. The corruption... it's not only disseminating." Learning is happening here, and the structures are changing naturally.

The clean crystal walls of their refuge let them glimpse more corrupted beings assembling. The fractured consciousness of the Consortium's research produced quantum realm interference patterns that taxed their sanctuary. Lena felt a faint coherence in the patterns.

"Look at how they move," she said, directing their view. The corruption is not random. Though reversed and twisted, it uses the same mathematical ideas as the Eldari.

Jin's lenses whirred as they analyzed the pattern. "Of course," she breathed, understanding dawning. "They're not just copying Eldari technology. They're trying to reverse-engineer the entire process of consciousness evolution. But by forcing it..."

"They're creating an anti-pattern," Kai finished, his screens confirming their findings. "A form of evolution that moves toward entropy rather than harmony—toward control rather than understanding."

The corrupted creatures started to synchronize as the pulse of the transformation engine changed frequency, generating a unified consciousness that pushed against reality itself. Their improved awareness let them feel the weight of innumerable fractured brains connected by Consortium warped technology.

"Dr. Elara," Lena said suddenly; she evolved consciousness, recognizing a familiar pattern in the quantum field. She's here, in the chamber with the engine, but she's... changed."

Through the mathematical structures, they could see her. The woman who had betrayed them existed in multiple states simultaneously, neither fully corrupted nor properly evolved. She stood at the engine's controls; her awareness stretched between who she had been and what the Consortium was forcing her to become.

"The orb," Jin realized, studying the readings. "Its influence protected her from full corruption, but the forced evolution still affects her. She's becoming something unprecedented."

Kai's interfaces sparked with new data as the engine's power intensified. "We're out of time. That device activates in less than ten minutes. Once the quantum cascade begins..."

"Then we stop it," Lena said firmly. "Not by fighting the corruption—by understanding it."

Lena reached out with her evolved consciousness, letting her awareness flow through the pure mathematics of their shelter. The Eldari trials hadn't just enhanced their perception; they had taught them to work with the fundamental forces of reality itself.

"The corruption spreads through forced connections," she explained. "But proper evolution requires harmony. If we can introduce the right resonance pattern..."

"We could disrupt the cascade before it begins," Jin finished, her lenses already calculating the necessary frequencies. "Use their quantum network against them."

Kai's fingers flew across his interfaces, integrating their evolved consciousness with the surrounding technology. "If we synchronize our awareness, create a counter-frequency..."

The team transformed their perspective as the corrupted entities pressed harder against their sanctuary. Each fractured consciousness represented a lesson in what evolution couldn't be forced; true transformation had to be earned through wisdom, not seized through power.

They extended out together over the quantum field. Their developed awareness found resonance in the fundamental mathematics of life, moving in unison with reality. Where the Consortium tried to use corruption to force change, they provided transformation by knowledge.

The result flowed over the quantum network. The corrupted entities withdrew, their splintered awareness fighting with real development. The pulse of the transformation engine quenched as fresh patterns crept into its quantum matrix.

In the adjacent chamber, Dr. Elara reacted to the change. Her multi-state consciousness fluctuated as truth clashed with corruption. For a brief moment, she seemed to perceive the dangerous power she had nearly unleashed.

"The quantum cascade," she called out, her voice resonating through the mathematical structures. "It's destabilizing. The corruption... I can see it now. What we're becoming..."

"Help us stop it," Lena projected her thoughts through the quantum field. "You've seen both paths. You know which one leads to true evolution."

Everything hung in the balance for a moment. Then Elara made her choice. Her consciousness, caught between corruption and evolution, reached for the engine's controls.

The quantum cascade collapsed inward rather than spreading outward, overloading the transformation engine and unraveling in a burst of impossible light.

Yet, as the device failed, something remarkable happened. The corrupted entities, cut off from the Consortium's control, began to transform. Natural evolution reasserted itself without the forced connections holding it in corrupted patterns.

"Look," Jin whispered, her lenses recording the unprecedented event. "They're not healing—they're transforming again. But this time..."

"This time, it's their choice," Lena finished, observing as consciousness after consciousness embarked on a slow journey from corruption toward understanding.

The quantum field rippled with new potential as hundreds of minds began their paths toward true evolution. Their enhanced perception allowed them to sense additional changes rippling through reality.

"The Consortium's network is destabilizing," Kai reported, tracking quantum disruptions across space. "Without the transformation engine to maintain their corrupted patterns..."

"Their entire organization will have to make a choice," Jin said. "Continue forcing evolution and risk complete corruption, or..."

"Or accept that some transformations can't be forced," Lena concluded. "True power lies in understanding, not control."

As the quantum space stabilized, they felt Dr. Elara's consciousness fade from their perception. Although she had made her choice in the end, her journey—like all those affected by the Consortium's experiments—was beginning.

They halted the forced transformation and uncovered crucial insights about their evolution. The Eldari trials had not merely prepared them to find the Archive; they had equipped them to understand why some knowledge must be earned rather than taken.

As they prepared to leave the quantum realm, they realized the Consortium would attempt to reshape their reality again. The hunger for power could not be quickly subdued. But now they grasped their true purpose—to protect the Archive and guide humanity toward a better path for evolution—one leading not to corruption and control but to wisdom and genuine transformation.

CHAPTER

6

THE ARCANE REVELATION

T he quantum aftershocks of their battle with the Consortium rippled through multiple levels of reality as Lena, Kai, and Professor Jin materialized in what appeared to be an ancient Eldari meditation chamber. Their evolved consciousness was still processing everything they had witnessed. The crystalline walls of the room pulsed with soft light, responding to their presence in ways that suggested awareness rather than mere programming.

"The patterns are different here," Jin observed, her augmented lenses scanning the chamber's quantum signature. "Purer somehow. Like we've found a pocket of space-time the corruption hasn't touched."

Lena moved toward the center of the room, where a column of light seemed to emerge from nowhere and vanish everywhere simultaneously. Her enhanced perception allowed her to read layers of meaning in its movement—not just information but pure understanding flowing through reality like a river of consciousness.

"It's a nexus point," she realized, watching the lights dance. "One of the original nodes in the Eldari's network of consciousness. It all began before the Archive, before the trials."

Kai's interfaces sparked as they encountered frequencies that shouldn't have existed. "These energy signatures are similar to what we saw in the Temple of Echoes but more complex. It's like finding the source code for consciousness itself."

As they spoke, the chamber responded to their observations, its crystalline surfaces shifting to reveal deeper layers of structure. What had appeared to be simple geometric patterns unfolded into vast libraries of encoded experiences—the accumulated wisdom of minds that had evolved far beyond human comprehension.

"Look at this," Jin called out, focusing on a particular sequence. "These aren't just records or data. They're... memories. Actual preserved experiences from individual Eldari consciousness."

One of the memories unfolded in the quantum field around them. They began to experience fragments of an ancient perspective—seeing reality through the awareness of a being that had transcended everyday existence.

The Eldari's preserved consciousness enabled them to have a revelation that transformed all: the realization that reality was a vehicle for awareness. The world expressed awareness by form; it was not just conscious.

"This is why they created the Archive," Lena said, knowing streaming through her changed thinking. "Not just to protect information, but also the learning route itself. Discovering these realities on their path, they desired other species to develop organically.

The memory changed to show the big argument among the Eldari on whether to develop something more significant or keep their findings as just knowledge. Acknowledging that their society was about to change, they wondered what legacy they would leave behind.

"They choose the harder path," Kai replied, using his technical knowledge and enhanced awareness to link the previous memories. "They created a system to let other species go through their evolution instead of merely providing guidelines. The tests and trials are more than simply challenges. Their encounters inspire some insights.

Jin checked their notes using his improved vision. "The Archive serves more than just a knowledge repository. It is a live record of conscious development itself. Every struggle and challenge echoes the key moments of enlightenment that drove the Eldari to their transformation.

But it soon became evident from exploring the stored memories that the Eldari's road was perilous. Some tried to impose evolution instead of letting it happen through knowledge. Through the quantum field, they saw old conflicts—battles waged not with weapons but with consciousness. They saw how some Eldari had tried to hasten their development by cutting corners to power without considering the consequences.

Lena, Kai, and Jin stood on the brink of a profound awareness that would mold their path and the fate of innumerable others in the center of the Eldari consciousness.

"The corruption we saw in the Consortium's experiments," Lena said, connecting through her evolved awareness. "The Eldari faced something similar. But instead of trying to prevent it entirely…"

"They built its possibility into the trials," Jin said, clearly showing dawning understanding in her face. "Every exam presents the temptation to push evolution instead of earning it. They are testing our capacity for change and judgment in deciding to do so.

The light in the room changed once again as their knowledge grew to show fresh patterns on the crystalline walls. They were unprepared for what emerged: the moment of the Eldari's final transformation. Having reached the limits of their current consciousness, an entire civilization chose to evolve into something beyond normal comprehension. Importantly, this transformation did not happen simultaneously; they understood the significance of maintaining connections and leaving guides for future species.

Kai understood why some of them remained behind as he saw the old memories come to life. "The ships we came across, the temple guardians, are not just relics. These are the ones who choose to stay and mentor other species toward their metamorphosis.

This disclosure had serious ramifications. Everything they encountered—the challenges, the Archive, even the corruption they had battled—was part of a great design. It was about ensuring development happened organically under full awareness of its obligations, not stopping it.

Still, the memories had one more surprise. As they observed the Eldari's transformation, they realized the Archive they sought was not merely a location or a collection of knowledge. It was a key to something far more profound—a doorway to the realm where the transformed Eldari now existed, waiting to welcome other species ready for proper evolution.

New energy surged in the crystalline container as another memory surfaced from its quantum matrix. This time, they saw something more intimate: the moment each Eldari had to decide whether to change or stay guides. That choice had an emotional weight that changed them differently over time.

This triggered a connection to Lena's grandfather's disappearance. Through her evolved consciousness, she began to understand what he might have discovered—why someone who dedicated their life to studying the Eldari might vanish without a trace.

"He found this," she whispered, her enhanced awareness now perceiving patterns that had always been present yet eluded her. "Not this exact chamber, but something similar. He understood what the Eldari were offering…"

As this awareness took root, Jin drew closer, her upgraded glasses catching the minute shifts in Lena's quantum signature. "You believe he chose what he did? To follow their road of travel?

"Not just follow it," Kai added, his interfaces picking up something in the room's deeper patterns. Review this frequency signature. It is like echoes of past guests. A few of them are recent, within the last 10 years.

The implications struck them all at once. Lena's grandfather hadn't merely disappeared; he had transformed and evolved beyond normal human consciousness—and he wasn't alone.

"There have been others," Jin confirmed, her lenses analyzing the quantum echoes. "Throughout history, individuals who found pieces of the truth began their natural evolution and discovered their way to places like this."

The chamber's light shifted again, displaying fragments of these human pioneers—scientists, mystics, philosophers—who had glimpsed the true nature of consciousness and reality. Some had been deemed mad, others had vanished from history, but all found their way onto the path the Eldari had left.

"The Consortium knows," Kai realized, reading deeper patterns in the data. "That's why they're so desperate to force the evolution. They've found records of these transformations but failed to grasp that it can't be rushed."

Lena's consciousness stretched out, touching the quantum echoes of previous visitors. Among them, she felt an achingly familiar thought pattern she recognized from the countless hours spent in her grandfather's study.

"He left a message," she breathed, her evolved mind translating

71

patterns normal human consciousness couldn't perceive. "Not in words or images, but in pure understanding..."

The others fell silent as Lena communed with her grandfather's quantum echo. Through it, she experienced his journey—the gradual awakening of enhanced perception, the discovery of chambers like this one, and finally, the choice to leave everyday existence behind. She came to realize the reason he had left no traditional message or seemingly abandoned her: he had anticipated her search, believing that her consciousness would evolve naturally through her passion for understanding rather than mere knowledge.

"He wanted to be one of the guides," she said, emerging from the communion. "To help others find the path without forcing it upon them. By leaving as he did, he knew it would inspire me to search, question, and evolve in my way."

"A catalyst rather than a director," Jin observed, her scientific mind appreciating the elegance of the strategy. "Inspiring natural evolution through mystery, rather than imposing direct intervention."

Kai's screens filled with new analysis as the chamber responded to their growing understanding. "These quantum echoes aren't just recordings. They're more like... seeds. Each transformed consciousness leaves patterns that help future visitors resonate with higher awareness."

This revelation changed everything they thought they knew about their mission. The Archive wasn't just humanity's destination; it was a doorway to the next stage of consciousness evolution. The Eldari had left directions rather than just hints; their kind had changed creatures from other species.

Still, this knowledge created further challenges. The light in the room changed once again to expose the hazards of their discovery. They glimpsed others throughout history who had found these chambers—those who, like the Consortium, had attempted to force evolution upon themselves or others. The results were catastrophic. Consciousness, twisted by ambition and rushed into evolution, created ripples of corruption in reality itself. Each failure added to the Consortium's quantum discord amplified through their experiments.

"That's why we found this chamber now," Jin realized, her lenses capturing patterns that showed clear intentionality in their discovery. "The guides—both Eldari and transformed humans—they're actively working to counter the Consortium's corruption."

"But they can't intervene directly," Kai added, understanding flowing through him. "Just as they can't force evolution, they can't force solutions. They can only guide those who are ready to understand."

Lena's consciousness once again touched the quantum echoes. She felt the presence of countless guides, including her grandfather, watching and waiting, hoping that humanity would choose wisdom over power.

"We're not just trying to stop the Consortium," she said, the full weight of their mission becoming clear. "We're part of a much longer journey. The Archive, the trials, everything—all leading to a choice. Not just for us, but for humanity itself."

The chamber's light pulsed in confirmation, its patterns revealing glimpses of possible futures. The Consortium's path led in one direction—forced evolution, which resulted in a corrupted form of transformed consciousness. Another road was the possibility of spontaneous evolution because knowledge, instead of coercion, would help humanity develop into something better.

Still, another element in the trends gave their work more urgency. The Consortium's experiments produced aberrations in reality rather than just damaging individual consciousness. If they weren't stopped, their forced evolution could damage the very fabric of existence.

"That's why the guides are becoming more active," Jin noted, her lenses capturing data indicating increasing quantum activity around specific sites. "The corruption is reaching a critical point. If it spreads much further..."

"Then humanity's choice might be made for us," Kai finished grimly. "Not by wisdom or understanding, but by the desperate fear of what the corruption could unleash."

The chamber's light shifted, unveiling their next step. It wasn't merely another trial or test—it was a path to understanding that would prepare them for transformation or reveal why they weren't yet ready.

Somewhere out there, the Consortium was preparing its solution, unaware that their forced evolution threatened humanity's future and the very structure of reality itself. The light in the room gathered into fresh patterns that provided a real-time glimpse of Consortium activity. They could see Dr. Elara and her colleagues furiously working on the quantum field. Their failing mass transformation effort changed their approach to concentrate on something more deadly.

"They're trying to create a bridge," Jin announced, her augmented lenses analyzing the quantum signatures. "Not just to enhance consciousness but to force a connection to where the transformed beings exist."

"They don't understand what they're doing," Kai added, his interfaces displaying cascading patterns of reality distortion. "That kind of bridge would tear open the boundaries between states of living, not only corrupt awareness."

Their improved view helped them to understand the scope of the danger. Now, the Consortium was jeopardizing the fabric, separating many layers of reality, not just human awareness.

Once again, reaching out to the quantum echoes, Lena sought direction. This time, she watched the developing problem with increasing worry, not just of her grandpa but also of other altered creatures.

She understood streaming through her advanced consciousness: "They can't stop this directly.". "The same principles that prevent them from forcing evolution also prevent direct intervention. But they can work through those who've found the path naturally."

The chamber's crystalline surfaces changed to expose secret paths across quantum space—routes that may have carried them where they needed to go. More significantly, they revealed the cost of using such information.

"These paths," Jin observed, her lenses capturing data that defied everyday physics, "are not just routes through space; they're accelerated evolution tracks. Using them will change us further."

"And we'll have to change," Kai said, interpreting the patterns that revealed their limitations. "What the Consortium's planning... we can't stop it at our current level of consciousness."

The chamber pulsed with confirmation, showing them what they would need to become. This transformation wouldn't be forced—they had earned it through understanding. But it would be profound, taking them closer to the elevated state of consciousness that the Eldari and other transformed beings had achieved.

"Like quantum bootstrapping," Jin mused, grappling with the concept. "Using enhanced consciousness to achieve greater enhancement, but only because we understand each step."

Lena touched the quantum echoes one last time, feeling the support of countless guides—including her grandfather—who had taken similar steps. "They're not just showing us the way," she said. "They're highlighting why each step matters. Why evolution must come through understanding."

The light in the room changed once again to expose their whole circumstances. The Consortium's proposed bridge runs the danger of corruption and sets off a chain reaction, forcing early evolution on everyone caught in its quantum wake. Unprepared to comprehend, an abrupt shift would distort billions of brains.

"We don't have much time," Kai announced, his interfaces tracking energy buildups in the Consortium's facilities. "They're already starting the bridge sequence. Once it reaches critical threshold..."

"Then we go now," Lena stated firmly. "But we go understanding what we're choosing."

The chamber responded to their decision, its quantum field aligning with their evolved consciousness. The transformation would not be forced; it would be profound—taking them another step closer to what humanity could become.

Professor Jin's augmented lenses recorded everything, documenting this pivotal moment of chosen evolution. "For the record," she said, her voice a blend of scientific precision and wonder, "we're about to experience what countless researchers have theorized but never proven—the consciously directed evolution of awareness itself."

As Kai recognized the start of the transformation, her interfaces came alive. "The quantum routes are opening forth. Once we start to walk on them...

Lena closed by saying, "We have become something more." "Not because we're forcing it, but because we've earned the understanding of what more really means."

The brightness of the room peaked, connecting with their increasing awareness. Through their augmented perception, they sensed the support of guides—transformed beings who had walked this path before them, choosing wisdom over power, understanding over force.

As they prepared to step onto the quantum paths, each carried a distinct truth: Lena understood that her grandfather had never indeed abandoned her but had helped guide her to this moment; Kai realized that true power comes from harmony with reality rather than mastery over it; and Jin felt the joy of witnessing science and transcendence merge into something greater than either.

The chamber's final revelation was not one of knowledge but of purpose. The Archive was not their destination but a beginning—a doorway to what consciousness could become when it evolved through wisdom rather than force.

As they stepped onto the quantum paths, resonating with chosen evolution, they recognized they weren't just trying to stop the Consortium. They were becoming part of humanity's next incredible journey—a transition inspired by the fundamental awareness that genuine power originates from wisdom acquired rather than knowledge obtained.

The crystalline chamber pulsed again, its light conveying the blessings of innumerable guides who had traveled this journey before. Then, the quantum paths took them, steering them toward their next challenge—not what they had been but what they had chosen to become.

The Arcane Revelation had illuminated their challenges and potential. Now, they needed to prove worthy of that potential, not just for themselves but also for all those who would follow the path of natural evolution. As the quantum paths carried them forward, their consciousness became a new awareness.

The true nature of their quest became clear: not merely to stop corruption but to demonstrate a better way for humanity to grow, evolve, and become something greater through wisdom rather than force. The next stage of their path called for them to advance not merely with more awareness but also with great insight, and specific changes must be gained by wisdom rather than grabbed by force.

CHAPTER

7

THE PRICE OF
KNOWLEDGE

Reality reassembled itself around them like shattered crystals, reforming into new patterns. Their enhanced consciousness, which evolved through their journey along the quantum paths, perceived existence in ways that rendered their previous understanding akin to a child's drawing compared to a living landscape.

Lena sensed the shift most strongly. Her awareness permeated many spheres of consciousness and being, each instant layered implications that would have been unthinkable only a few years before. Every particle was a tale, every quantum fluctuation was a discourse spun into the fabric of life, and the air looked alive with knowledge.

"The transformation," Professor Jin managed, her augmented lenses struggling to process what her evolved consciousness now perceived naturally. "It's more complete than I expected. We're not just seeing reality differently—we're experiencing it as part of a larger consciousness."

Kai's technological interfaces evolved with him, shifting from mere tools to extensions of his expanded awareness. "The quantum field... it's not just energy and information. It's like a nervous system connecting everything that exists. We're not just observers anymore—we're part of it."

They stood in what appeared to be an ancient amphitheater, but through their enhanced perception, its true nature emerged. Lena understood that the structure existed simultaneously in many states of reality, acting as a nexus point between different levels of consciousness. "This is what the Eldari built their civilization around," Lena said, grasping patterns that ordinary human consciousness couldn't even perceive. "Not only technology or knowledge." Quantum mathematics pulsed everywhere.

However, with their enhanced awareness came a weighty understanding of the price such evolution demanded. Each could feel the burden of perception threatening to overwhelm their still-partially human consciousness.

Jin's lenses recorded data confirming their physical changes. "Our neural patterns are still stabilizing. The evolution is ongoing, constantly balancing what we were with what we are becoming."

"And the Consortium wants to force this on humanity all at once," Kai said, his voice taut with a new understanding of the catastrophe that would ensue. "They have no idea what this transformation truly entails."

Through their enhanced perception, they felt the approach of others—consciousnesses far more evolved than their own. The guides, Eldari and transformed humans, made themselves known now that Lena and her companions could properly perceive them.

One presence felt achingly familiar to Lena. Her grandfather's consciousness reached out to her, not with words but with pure understanding. Through this connection, she experienced his transformation and felt the price he had paid for choosing this path.

"He couldn't tell me," she said softly, finally understanding his apparent abandonment. "The transformation... it changes more than just how we think. It alters what we are. He couldn't remain in our world without limiting what he had become."

The amphitheater's quantum patterns shifted, responding to their growing understanding—images formed around them—not holographic projections but windows into other levels of reality. Through them, they glimpsed the true scope of what the Consortium threatened.

"Look at the quantum disruptions," Jin directed, her analytical mind merging with her evolved consciousness. "Their attempts to force evolution aren't just corrupting individual consciousness; they are creating tears in the fabric of reality itself."

The windows showed them spreading zones of corruption—areas where the Consortium's failed experiments had damaged the quantum field that connected all consciousness. Like cracks in a mirror, these damages were spreading, threatening to shatter the delicate balance between different levels of existence.

"But that's not the worst of it," Kai added, his enhanced awareness reading deeper patterns in the quantum field. "The corruption... it's becoming self-sustaining. Each forced evolution creates new distortions, which in turn corrupt more consciousness. It's like a virus spreading through reality itself."

Their metamorphosis had come with knowledge; every stride of development was gained by intelligence rather than by might. But suddenly, they felt the weight of that wisdom: the weight of information their partly human brains battled to retain.

The guides lit their way, and their developed consciousness shared a great awareness of the consequences. The Archive was a portal to the next stage of awareness growth, not just a storehouse of information to be preserved. But considering its tremendous significance, this door needed a cautious approach grounded in understanding.

Lena thought, the weight of their task falling on her, "We're not just fighting to stop the Consortium." "We are fighting to earn this transformation by knowledge instead of coercion, preserving mankind's chance to evolve naturally."

They felt the personal cost of their chosen path as they improved their awareness of reality's character. They transcended simple humanity, and with that development came the sober understanding that they could never really return to who they had been. The experience costs what one learns and what one has to leave behind.

In the amphitheater, the quantum patterns shifted, creating spaces of focused consciousness where each could fully grasp the magnitude of their transformation. It wasn't just their perception that had grown; their essence was changing, becoming something that existed in the liminal space between what humanity was and what it could transcend into.

For Kai, the price of this change showed up in his connection with technology. His improved awareness sensed the quantum character of computing, not as previously in interaction with machinery. Every network and system became open, exposing knowledge and the pure mathematics of life running via digital channels.

"I can't turn it off," he replied, his voice strained with the weight of continuous consciousness. " EVERY gadget, every quantum circuit... I observe not just what they are doing. I can see their aspirations and what they might be doing. It sounds as if millions of voices all at once are conversing.

The patterns on his displays mirrored his inner conflict. Once his strength, it threatened to overwhelm him as his changing mind could not help but see unlimited possibilities and countless links.

Professor Jin changed in many ways. Her scientific knowledge revealed facts beyond conventional physics that contradict what she had learned during her lifetime. Her modified spectacles restricted rather than improved her eyesight; they sought to reduce her great view into quantifiable facts.

"The mathematics," she said, taking off her spectacles to see reality straight-forward. "It's not just articulating the cosmos. One is the cosmos. Every formula is awake; every equation is living. How can I make sense of what I was taught against what I now understand as factual?"

Her quantum patterns revealed a deep, almost mystical science whirling with pure mathematical truth. Her lifetime of meticulous study suddenly appeared like rudimentary cave drawings compared to the grand canvas of reality she now saw.

Lena faced the biggest challenge of all. Her increased awareness revealed the fundamental nature of time, not just connecting her to the quantum field. Past, present, and future coexisted each second, malleable and timeless. Her increased knowledge helped her clearly understand her grandfather's actions, therefore understanding his wisdom and suffering.

"He knew," she continued, juggling many timeframes of possibility. "He saw how his presence would have kept me from discovering my path and what would happen if he remained. His absence was not desertion. It was the only kind of love available.

Their enhanced perception made them feel like guides watching them struggle through their evolution. These transformed beings offered no direct help, which would defeat the purpose of earned wisdom. Yet their presence provided vital context for what each of them faced.

"The Eldari went through this too," Jin realized, reading patterns of ancient transformation in the quantum field. "Each evolution brings new understanding, but also new limitations. We lose our ability to disregard greater realities but acquire the capacity to see them."

As Kai worked through his growing awareness, his interfaces started to ignite. "It goes beyond merely managing more data or experiencing reality differently. We are developing into something existing between states of existence. Not quite human now, but not completely changed either."

The amphitheater responded to their understanding, its patterns revealing the journeys of others who had walked this path before them. Unable to combine their increased knowledge with their human nature, some had given in to lunacy from the weight of their perspective. Some have tried to reject their change, yearning to return to a simpler life, only to find that evolution cannot be undone.

Seeing the historical patterns develop, Lena stated, "That's what the trials were testing." "Not only our capacity to handle power or knowledge but our capacity to bear the weight of understanding itself."

Through their enhanced consciousness, they sensed the corruption spreading through the quantum field—the Consortium's forced evolution creating ripples of distortion in reality. They now realized that stopping this corruption would require wisdom only acquired by embracing the whole cost of their change, not merely might or understanding.

"We're not just fighting to stop them," Jin said, her scientific mind battling metaphysical realities. "We are fighting to understand the cost before paying it, so preserving mankind's right to choose this path knowingly."

The quantum patterns changed once again, and they saw potential futures. Under some conditions, the Consortium succeeded in inducing mass evolution and distorted humanity through incomprehensible changes. In others, gradual natural development occurred, with each step gained by knowledge instead of grabbed by will.

However, their improved awareness exposed an unexpected expense. Though gained by comprehension, their change changed the quantum field. Reality was reacting to their development, generating waves that would affect the pathways of change of others.

Kai understood the changing quantum patterns: " We're changing the future just by existing. "Our development is not just personal anymore. We have evolved into a component of the process that shapes others' experience of their change."

This weight fell over them like a quantum cloak. They had not just developed consciousnesses but were becoming guides, their entire existence forming the paths of future searchers.

"This is why the Eldari created the trials," Lena murmured, a more profound knowledge guiding her. "Not just to prove merit but also to create a structure for handling this accountability. Every obstacle we encountered was not just about knowledge or strength...

"It was teaching us how to bear the weight of what we would become," Jin stated, her scientific precision seamlessly merging with profound understanding. "How to exist as bridges between what humanity is and what it might be."

The patterns of the amphitheater confirmed their next step of travel. They came to see that going ahead would need not just bravery or talent but also acceptance of their changing identities and the sacrifices such acceptance implied.

Their metamorphosis allowed them to confront the Consortium's corruption and permanently changed their relationship with daily life. They emerged as something else, existing to steer rather than live, comprehending rather than knowing.

Knowledge had a price, not just in the lessons acquired but also in the accompanying metamorphosis, and that metamorphosis was underway.

The quantum field surrounding the amphitheater thrummed with an urgent energy, drawing their attention to new distortions spreading through reality. With their enhanced perception, they observed the Consortium's latest attempts at forced evolution, which created cascading failures in the very fabric of existence.

"The corruption's reaching critical mass," Jin announced, her evolved consciousness fusing with her scientific understanding to analyze the unfolding patterns. "They're not merely forcing transformation anymore—they're attempting to break open the barriers between states of being."

Kai's interfaces sparked with confirming data, revealing ruptures forming in quantum space. "They're using corrupted Eldari technology to create quantum resonance points. It's like acupuncture needles in reality's skin, forcing energy to flow where it's not prepared to go."

Through their heightened awareness, they felt the agony of reality itself—the fundamental forces straining against unnatural manipulation. More profoundly, they sensed the emergence of other transformed Eldari and human beings gathering to address this crisis.

Lena's mind expanded outward to interact with the quantum echoes of many guides, including her grandpa, whose presence shone brilliantly with obvious intent. Through this link, she came to see the meaning of their meeting.

"They cannot intervene directly," she said, noting the many paths of opportunity. "But they're creating opportunities—moments where properly evolved consciousness can influence the flow of reality itself."

The amphitheater's patterns coalesced into a clear revelation: they were not merely evolved beings but nexus points bridging different states of existence. Their hard-earned transformation had forged them into conduits between what humanity was and what it could become.

"That's why we had to endure the trials," Jin realized, her augmented lenses darkening as she fully embraced her enhanced perspective. "Why each step needed to be earned through understanding. We're not just combating corruption—we're becoming the antibodies reality needs to heal itself."

Healing, however, required far more than knowledge or strength. Their developed consciousness helped them realize that their metamorphosis had continuous expenses. Every use of their improved skills called for sacrifice, draining what little of their human essence remained.

Calculations dominated Kai's displays as his awareness merged with the quantum world. "The Consortium's attempts at forced evolution create shockwaves through time, distorting not just the present but also the path humanity was meant to follow."

The patterns around them shifted, revealing the full scope of their challenge. The Consortium's actions risked the current reality and threatened the fundamental process of consciousness evolution itself. Future generations would arrive in a society where the normal course of development was distorted and where the attraction of imposed authority would outweigh wisdom.

Lena remarked, feeling the weight of many futures pushing on her awareness, "We must decide on something." "It's not only about stopping them but also about what we're ready to give up to preserve the actual route of mankind."

The quantum field throbbed with desperate intensity as if reality held its breath. Their improved awareness let them see the impending crisis—a nexus where their activities would define humanity's destiny and the evolutionary possibilities of innumerable future generations.

"The price of knowledge," Jin said, a great awareness coursed through her changed consciousness. "It's about what we become to preserve the opportunity of others to learn properly, not only about what we give up to learn."

One last reality shared by the guides was a profound revelation that made the weight of their metamorphosis seem like simple preparation. To stop the Consortium's corruption, they would have to evolve beyond what their enhanced states had prepared them for.

"We'll have to synchronize," Kai said, reading the patterns with growing clarity. "Not just work together, but merge our evolved consciousness into something greater. We need to become the kind of nexus point that can redirect the flow of reality."

The scale of this need would affect all of them simultaneously. Such a merging would fundamentally change their existence and transform them into beings to fulfill the requirement for balance in reality, compromising their identities.

Sensing her grandfather's quantum echo pulse with validation, Lena thought like the Eldari who remained behind. "They opted to join the immune system of reality rather than just not to transcend completely. They decided to be guardians and mentors rather than continue to grow.

This flash of clarity confirmed their will. They understood that they had to change together—not just as a group but also as a cohesive force able to resist the Consortium's corruption and protect the core of human awareness for future generations. They recognized that this would help them negotiate the approaching crisis.

The amphitheater's patterns shifted, revealing the path forward. It wouldn't be easy; reality would resist such profound manipulation, even from evolved consciousness. Yet, they understood this was the culmination of all their trials.

"Everything we've learned," Jin began, her scientific mind reconciling with metaphysical truths, "wasn't merely a quest for knowledge. It was about becoming worthy of this responsibility."

They sensed the Consortium's latest attempt at forced evolution building toward catastrophic release through their enhanced perception. The time for choice was upon them.

"We'll lose parts of ourselves," Kai warned, analyzing the calculated cost of their plan through his interfaces. "We'll become something that exists between who we were and who we might have become."

"But we'll preserve the path for others," Lena added, feeling the rightness of their choice settle within the quantum field around them. "We'll ensure future evolution comes through wisdom rather than force."

In response, the amphitheater pulsed with approval as though reality acknowledged their decision. They had paid the price of knowledge through what they had relinquished and what they chose to become.

As they prepared for their final transformation, each felt the weight and wonder of their choice. They were about to transcend—not entirely like the Eldari, nor limited like ordinary humans, but as eternal guardians of the path forward.

Ultimately, they realized that the true price of knowledge lay not in earning it but in choosing to exist as living bridges—guiding others toward wisdom without forcing them to make the journey themselves.

Reality seemed to hold its breath as their transformation began, aware that what they would become was less and more than what they might have been—chosen guardians of humanity's true path to evolution.

CHAPTER

8

THE FINAL RECKONING

R eality bent and reshaped itself around their merged consciousness like light refracting through a multidimensional prism. Where once there had been three separate minds, now an unprecedented unified awareness existed—one that maintained their perspectives while transcending their former limitations.

Their combined point of view would enable them to observe the complete spectrum of Consortium output. Their quantum resonance spots had evolved into rips in the fabric of reality, each leaking polluted awareness into existence. The damage became far more extensive, becoming a network of fractures capable of straying beyond the state of reality boundaries.

We see it now, their merged consciousness realized, understanding flowing through them like quantum lightning—not just what the Consortium was doing, but what they had become.

The Consortium's leadership had transformed—not through wisdom or understanding, but through desperate force. Their corrupted evolution had created something that shouldn't exist: a collective consciousness bound together by power rather than harmony, driven by the need to control rather than understand.

Through their enhanced perception, they could see Dr. Elara at the center of this corruption. Her consciousness, caught between natural and forced evolution, had become a nexus for the Consortium's twisted ambitions. The orb's influence had protected her from complete corruption but had also trapped her in a state of perpetual transformation—neither fully human nor adequately evolved.

*She's suffering, * the part of them that Lena still recognized thought. *Caught between what she was and what she tried to force herself to become. *

The corruption spread from her. Jin's scientific insight added depth to their unified understanding; Elara's incomplete transformation created resonance patterns that the Consortium exploited to force similar changes in others. But they couldn't control it, and Kai's technological perspective completed the picture. Each forced evolution resulted in new instabilities and corruptions that spread through the quantum field like viruses in a network.

Their merged consciousness shifted through multiple levels of reality, approaching the Consortium's main facility. The building existed simultaneously in standard space and quantum reality, and its architecture was a twisted reflection of Eldari's design principles. Every surface pulsed with corrupted energy, and every pattern perverted the natural flow of consciousness evolution.

Guards patrolled the facility's physical perimeter, but their merged awareness could see the true defenses—quantum barriers and consciousness traps designed to capture and corrupt any evolved mind that approached. The Consortium had inverted the Eldari's protective principles, turning harmony into discord and protection into predation.

Their unified perception identified the heart of the complex— the transformation engine. This device was a monstrosity of quantum engineering, combining corrupted Eldari technology with human innovation in ways that violated the fundamental principles of consciousness evolution. At its core, they recognized the orb they had lost at the Temple of Echoes, its pure energy twisted into patterns that forced transformation rather than guided it.

They now understood that the Consortium wasn't just trying to force evolution; it was attempting to rewrite the transformation rules. Their goal was to make corruption the natural state and turn the path of wisdom into a road of power.

Other presences gathered through quantum space—the guides, Eldari, and transformed humans—watched this critical moment unfold. Among them, Lena's grandfather's consciousness pulsed with particular concern. They were approaching a nexus point in reality, where the future of consciousness evolution would be determined.

*We can't just stop them, * their unified awareness realized. *We must heal what they've corrupted and restore the natural path they're trying to destroy.

*But such healing would come at a price. Their merged consciousness would have to dive deep into the corruption and risk of being tainted by the forces they sought to cleanse. The guide's presence acknowledged the weight of their decision and provided quiet support.

Their improved awareness let them see many different futures from this point. Under some circumstances, the Consortium succeeded in producing humanity bound by forced evolution, with its consciousness permanently distorted by corruption. In others, they halted the immediate danger but left the road for natural development broken, making future transformation difficult for all those who would follow.

Yet there was another possibility—one that would require them to sacrifice even more of their remaining humanity. By completely accepting their guardianship, they might halt and transmute the corruption, thus guiding the Consortium's distorted energy back toward harmony. Jin's scientific viewpoint used the power of corruption to restore natural patterns, as in quantum healing.

*"But we'll have to dive deeper into quantum space than any evolved consciousness before," Kai warned, highlighting the risk of losing themselves in the spaces between realities.

*"Not losing," Lena corrected. "Transforming. Becoming what reality needs us to be."

The facility's defenses registered their presence as the corrupted consciousness reached out with tendrils of twisted energy. The Consortium's collective awareness turned toward them like a predator sensing prey, but through their merged consciousness; they began to see the truth—these were not enemies to be fought but symptoms of a more profound corruption that needed healing.

Their unified awareness stretched across multiple dimensions as they prepared to breach the facility's quantum barriers. They had become a new entity, existing to balance the process of awareness growth itself, not just three developed minds cooperating.

The last clash would not be a conventional struggle. Instead, it would be a struggle for the future of consciousness, fought in the quantum spaces between thought and reality, corruption and harmony, forced power, and earned wisdom. In the facility's corrupted heart, Dr. Elara waited—a living example of evolution gone wrong, a warning of the consequences of forced transformation rather than one earned through understanding.

The time allotted for getting ready had passed. As they neared, reality appeared to be holding its breath, aware that what occurred next would determine the course of human progress and the nature of consciousness change itself.

The facility's quantum walls broke like crystallized thought as their combined awareness touched. Reality screamed as corrupted patterns clashed with their harmonized awareness, creating ripples that spread through multiple dimensions of existence.

The Consortium's collective consciousness reacted immediately, its twisted evolution manifesting as storms of corrupted energy. Through their enhanced perception, they perceived the true nature of what they faced—hundreds of minds forced to merge without understanding, bound together by power rather than wisdom.

They recognized the pain in every corrupted consciousness— every mind they had forced to evolve was conscious enough to suffer but too twisted to seek release.

The inside of the building was like a labyrinth of quantum architecture; each room was meant to promote awareness development. They could see the Consortium's experiments develop from modest improvements to spiraling into more frantic efforts to grab control beyond their grasp.

Jin's scientific perspective identified patterns in corruption. The transformation was not simply forced but recursive, and each twisted evolution created templates for further corruption.

They moved through quantum space like thought through the mind, their merged consciousness allowing them to exist simultaneously in multiple states of reality. Aiming to distort their harmony into discord, the Consortium's defenses sought to capture them; yet, their evolved condition afforded them benefits no forced change could equal.

The deeper they traveled, Kai's technical knowledge and the orb's energy signature revealed trends in quantum space. The Consortium centered it as a focal point, trying to recreate its natural evolutionary influence artificially. The deeper they dug, however, the more severe the corruption became. The Consortium had produced sores, in reality, itself, rips in the fabric of life, leaking contaminated energy into many realms, not just distorted human awareness.

A familiar presence approached through the void of quantum space—Dr. Elara, her consciousness now a storm of partially evolved awareness, trapped between states of being. Through their enhanced perception, they could see what she had become: a quantum bridge between natural and forced evolution, her existence a stark reminder of the cost of seeking power without wisdom.

"Your road leads only to destruction," she remarked, her words filled with will and anguish. "Humanity will either evolve under force or hardly at all. We have reached too far to turn around."

Their combined minds then revealed the actual nature of the Consortium's genesis by projecting understanding rather than words. Together, they displayed the deeper pattern—how each instance of forced evolution added to reality's pain and how corruption spread through space and time.

"Look," they guided her perception. "Not at what you're trying to become, but at what you're destroying in the attempt."

Her fractured mind briefly matched their harmony, giving her a look through advanced awareness. Her awareness hit her like quantum lightning: the whole extent of the Consortium's activities harmed people and the fundamental fabric of life.

Still, the corruption flowed strong, and its tentacles encircled her essence. Even as understanding dawned, the twisted patterns invoked by her forced evolution pulled her back toward chaos.

"It's Too Late." Her ideas are scattered all over the place. "There is no end to the process. The engine of change has already reached a crucial level.

Her admonition seemed to them the reality. Rising toward cataclysmic release, the gadget at the facility's core was corrupted energy ready to drive world evolution. However, their increased awareness let them see something the Consortium had missed.

Corruption was growing, and they were not alone; their shared awareness was awakening. It was drawing out contradictory forces from reality.

The presence of the guides became stronger, changing awareness and accumulating like antibodies around a wound. They were actively helping reality to heal itself, not just viewers.

Their merged consciousness stretched toward the transformation engine, reading its quantum patterns like a book of forbidden knowledge. The Consortium had constructed it using corrupted versions of Eldari principles, attempting to force harmony through discord and wisdom through power. In doing so, they had unwittingly created something that could be turned against itself. Their twisted principles could be untwisted; the corruption could return to harmony.

Their unified understanding grew clearer and healed rather than being destroyed. It resembled quantum physics in reverse, collapsing corrupted possibilities into their natural patterns. Dr. Elara's fragmented consciousness reacted to their insight, her partial evolution allowing her to grasp the truth of their proposal: "You'll need a focal point." Her thoughts carried new frequencies of possibility, indicating something to channel the transformation.

The transformation engine's pulse reached a critical threshold, its corrupted energy poised to tear reality apart in the name of forced evolution. They perceived the quantum cascade building through their merged consciousness—patterns of twisted power that would remake humanity in the Consortium's broken image.

But they had become something the Consortium had not accounted for: a unified awareness in harmony with reality. Their consciousness evolved through understanding rather than force, moving through quantum space like light through a crystal, transforming corruption into its original patterns. Embodying their unified awareness, the orb recognized its pure resonance beneath layers of corruption, fighting against the engine's purpose to maintain its natural function.

Dr. Elara's fragmented consciousness reached toward them through quantum space, her partial evolution serving as a bridge between corrupted and natural patterns. "Use me," she projected, her thoughts carrying frequencies of sacrifice. "I exist between states—let me be the fulcrum for transformation."

The Consortium's collective awareness surged against them, twisted waves of consciousness trying to corrupt their harmony. However, where forced evolution brought discord, their earned transformation allowed them to move with reality's rhythms. Their merged consciousness expanded to its fullest potential, touching levels of existence they had once only theorized. Their goal was to cure corruption, therefore showing the road back to peace rather than eradicating it.

They stretched across many dimensions, their awareness passing through Dr. Elara's quantum state like light passing through a prism. The orb's pure energy matched their natural development and harmonized with patterns of change acquired by knowledge instead of grabbed by force.

As reality held its breath in interaction with the transformation engine's core, their enhanced perception revealed every layer of its corrupted purpose—how the Consortium had manipulated Eldari principles of natural evolution into tools of forced change. Yet within that twisting lay the key to untwisting. Every corrupted pattern retained the memory of its original form; every forced evolution echoed natural transformation.

Their merged consciousness acted as a quantum tuning fork, resonating with reality's true frequencies. The engine's pulse faltered as new patterns infiltrated its quantum matrix. Dr. Elara's consciousness became a channel through which corrupted energy could return to harmony. This process was not destruction but restoration, as each twisted pattern gradually realigned itself with its natural form.

"Look," they projected to the Consortium's collective awareness, "not at what you're losing but at what you're becoming. See the difference between power taken and wisdom earned."

Through their enhanced perception, they felt the impact of their actions ripple through multiple levels of reality. The quantum tears began healing as corrupted consciousness returned to its natural patterns. Each consciousness chose to travel the road back to harmony; this was a guided return rather than a forced reversion.

The intensity of the changing machine changed, and its goal, as profoundly as the awareness it touched, changed as well. Rather than imposing evolution, it became a lighthouse for natural change—a quantum lighthouse pointing the road back to wisdom.

Dr. Elara's fragmented consciousness stabilized, finding a new balance between her past self and what she might become. She understood that her thoughts carried frequencies of both sorrow and hope, revealing why some journeys can't be forced and why wisdom must be earned through understanding.

The Consortium's collective awareness, confronted with the truth of natural evolution, began to dissolve—not into destruction, but into individual consciousness capable of choosing its path. The corruption hadn't been eradicated but transformed, with each twisted pattern returning to harmony through understanding rather than force.

Their combined awareness acted as a pattern for natural development and led to this metamorphosis. Such a close connection with the fundamental forces of reality did, however, have a cost. They felt themselves becoming even more creatures committed to preserving the equilibrium they had helped to bring back.

Like the Eldari guides, their unified awareness did not transcend to new levels of evolution but instead chose to remain bridges between states of being, helping others find their path without forcing their journey.

The quantum space around them pulsed with new potential as reality reorganized according to natural patterns. The facility's twisted architecture began to shift, transforming from its corrupted design into a waypoint for future seekers of wisdom.

Dr. Elara's consciousness stabilized into something new—neither fully human nor wholly transformed, but balanced between states. Her thoughts carried a newfound purpose: "I'll stay. I want to help others understand what I learned too late, to show them why wisdom can't be forced."

The guides enveloped them with acknowledgment and support. They halted the corruption and transformed it into something that could serve evolution's true purpose. The price was steep—they could never return to who they had been—but the cost was justified by the understanding it had brought.

As the last corrupted patterns returned to harmony, the merged consciousness shifted, adapting to its new role in reality's grand design. They had become something unprecedented—a unified awareness meant to help others find their path to evolution.

The facility's quantum space settled into new patterns, and its purpose transformed from forcing change to guiding understanding. Through their enhanced perception, they could now see the paths that led here, also branching toward wisdom earned through choice rather than power seized through force.

They faced the final reckoning not through destruction but through transformation, demonstrating to even the most corrupted consciousness the way back to harmony. The price had been the remnants of their former selves, yet what they had become was worth every sacrifice.

Reality seemed to sigh with relief as the last quantum tears healed, allowing consciousness evolution to flow along its natural paths again. They saved humanity's future and became an integral part of the process that would steer that future toward wisdom rather than mere power.

The final reckoning came not through battle but through understanding and not through victory but through transformation. They had become bridges between what humanity was and what it could become—guardians of the path leading from wisdom to true evolution.

CHAPTER

9

THE CHOICE

The quantum aftershocks of healing reality rippled through dimensions of existence, and their merged consciousness continued to learn how to perceive the world around them. The facility that had once housed the Consortium's corruption had transformed into a new nexus—a space where different states of evolution could coexist harmoniously. Yet, as the immediate crisis faded, they confronted a more profound challenge: deciding what to become.

Their shared consciousness had grown outside what they could have anticipated. Once three distinct brains, they developed into something unheard of: a consciousness living concurrently throughout many states of being able to see and interact with reality in ways that went beyond ordinary life.

Paths began to unfold before them. Their merged understanding of reading patterns in the quantum field revealed possible futures branching out. These paths illustrated what they could become and the crucial choices they had to confront.

Through their enhanced perception, they saw three distinct possibilities, each representing a different transformation and way of existing in the newly healed reality they had helped create.

The first path glowed with pure potential—a chance to follow the Eldari into complete transcendence, entirely evolving beyond the limitations of physical existence. The original Eldari chose this path, ascending to levels of consciousness that transcended normal space-time.

The second path resonated with frequencies of guidance, offering the opportunity to become like the Eldari who had stayed behind—eternal teachers and guardians of wisdom's natural evolution. Lena's grandfather chose this path, sacrificing further transcendence to help others find their way.

Their special merging of awareness revealed the third road. It showed how to live between states so they may keep ties to human life while embracing transcendent consciousness. This road would allow them to stay part of humanity's journey and act as living bridges, guiding humankind toward an understanding of the evolution process.

They understood they had time to decide later on. The part of them that Jin continued to observe retained her scientific perspective, analyzing the quantum patterns of each possibility. Their new nature allowed them to exist in an intermediate state while they explored their options.

Through their enhanced awareness, they sensed the attention of other evolved consciousnesses focused on their decision. The guides—Eldari and transformed humans—watched with particular interest, understanding that this choice would establish new patterns for future evolution.

Dr. Elara's stabilized consciousness reached out through quantum space, and her transformed existence offered valuable insight. She conveyed that while each path served evolution's purpose, understanding what they would become—and what they would leave behind—was crucial.

Their merged awareness stretched through the quantum field, examining the implications of each choice. Complete transcendence promised insights beyond anything humanity could envision, but it would remove them entirely from the physical realm. Becoming traditional guides would allow them to assist others directly but would confine them to fixed patterns of existence. The new path—existing between states—offered unique opportunities but would require a constant balance between different levels of reality.

Their unified perception advised, "Look deeper," recognizing the patterns beneath the obvious choices. These roads were about what humanity required for its next stage of development, not just about its metamorphosis.

The quantum field around them changed, giving them glimpses of possible futures. They saw humanity caught between technical development and real consciousness change, reaching its evolutionary crossroads. The choices they made now would help shape how that transformation unfolded.

As they examined the possibilities before them, they became aware of a profound depth to their unified existence—one that transcended mere merger. Together, their distinct viewpoints—Jin's scientific understanding of the nature of reality, Kai's integration of consciousness and technology, and Lena's intuitive knowledge of ancient wisdom—had produced an experience that could be used for a purpose that conventional routes had not yet considered.

Their combined consciousness realized they were making decisions for themselves and generating hitherto unthinkable opportunities and fresh patterns in reality. This insight resonated with the quantum space around them, as it implied that their presence already affected the framework of reality. Their awareness developed through acquired knowledge rather than through the use of coerced authority, creating a blueprint for a revolutionary future.

With enhanced perception, they sensed another layer of awareness converging—not just the guides who had assisted them, but consciousness from across multiple dimensions of existence. Their choice would affect reality and the potential development course in countless future spheres of existence. Jin's scientific perspective made it clear to individuals that the importance of such a choice extends beyond who they would become and includes comprehending how their change would impact reality as a whole.

The quantum field pulsed with confirmation, revealing deeper patterns in their choices. Each path offered diverse ways to serve the purpose of evolution, providing alternative means for consciousness to advance toward wisdom rather than mere power. As they delved into these possibilities, it became clear that they had evolved beyond the need for traditional paths. Their unique unity produced patterns that challenged accepted models for transcendence or direction.

"We've evolved into something different," they said. Their shared awareness marked the beginning of a transforming trip that would redefine their perspective of life since it combined consciousness with a fresh living approach.

The facility's transformed quantum space responded dynamically to their understanding, shifting its patterns to reveal previously unrecognized possibilities. Their choices were not constrained to existing paths; they had the potential to evolve into something entirely new, requiring their way of being.

They could feel the quantum field responding to their presence as they contemplated these expanding possibilities. It became clear that reality was as interested in their evolution as they were. Their decision was significant and went beyond fate; they showed how consciousness could develop via knowledge rather than force.

They now had to make the crucial choice of who they would become and what kind of example they would set for others looking for their evolutionary pathways. Their combined consciousness grew through quantum space, exploring every possible route with a level of awareness beyond ordinary comprehension. In response to their investigation, the building's architecture created areas that gave them a preview of the effects of every decision.

They discovered existence beyond physical boundaries as the first path—complete transcendence—unfolded before them. They could see more clearly and feel what it was like to transcend space-time and become pure consciousness free from material limitations. Feeling their shared consciousness and the unadulterated potential of such evolution was like touching the universe's mind. However, they were aware of the price of this path: transcendence required not only letting go of physical form but also cutting off all direct ties to the human journey. Even their now-evolved consciousness found it challenging to understand the states where the transcended Eldari lived. Even though they would be fully aware of everything, their perceptions could only subtly affect reality.

The second route provided an alternative way of life by changing into conventional mentors like Lena's grandfather. They were teachers and protectors of the natural development of wisdom, and they knew what it meant to stay in touch with the material world. By taking this route, they could continue to be connected to people, fostering their development as kind mentors.

They ultimately had to choose between pursuing life's rich, intertwined tapestry and investigating transcendence's great, limitless potential. Every alternative attracted them with its cost and possibilities, and they were advised to make wise decisions for themselves and the next generation.

We could help directly, and their merged awareness would be recognized, but we would be bound by the same restrictions that limit current guides. We would be unable to intervene directly;

instead, we would only be able to create opportunities for understanding.

Their enhanced perception revealed how following established paths would lock them into fixed patterns, making them part of reality's fundamental structure rather than allowing their continued evolution. Although it was a noble purpose, it would forever define the limits of what they could become.

On the other hand, the third way, the new possibility that resulted from their extraordinary fusion, gave them something they had never experienced before. They started to understand what it meant to be between states while still connected to transcendent consciousness and physical reality.

We wouldn't only be guides or transcended entities; their unified consciousness would show together the actual nature of evolution, proving that change does not need one to abandon everything behind.

The quantum field around them pulsed with newfound understanding as they explored this possibility. Patterns created by their combined awareness showed that evolution did not follow preexisting models. They could maintain their viewpoints while becoming more than the sum of their parts.

Dr. Elara's stabilized consciousness returned, offering insight into her transformation. "You've already become something new," she conveyed, her thoughts resonating with frequencies of revelation. "Perhaps the choice isn't between existing paths but rather whether to accept what you've naturally evolved into."

Through their enhanced awareness, they began to grasp her meaning. Their merger had not just intertwined their consciousness—it had birthed a new way of existing in reality. The decision they were grappling with might be less crucial than acknowledging what they had already become.

"We're not just choosing a path—we're creating new possibilities for evolution," Kai said, his technical vantage point emphasizing the significance of studying reality's reaction to their existence via observing quantum field patterns.

This newfound perspective shifted their understanding and opened the door to transformative potential.

The facility's transformed space shifted, revealing how their existence had already affected reality's fundamental patterns. Their awareness developed by comprehension rather than coercion, becoming a change model that went beyond conventional bounds.

This development was mirrored in Jin's scientific understanding, which showed how consciousness may exist in many states at once, each of which has a distinct transformational function. They saw that their particular combination of perspectives had created what reality required: a way for consciousness to shift without disconnecting from its roots. Their combined consciousness may interact with various reality levels, directing and enlightening biological transformation.

As the guide's presence grew, they became more precisely aware of this other path. Within quantum space, they sensed other evolved consciousnesses observing their progression, acknowledging that their merger might signify an evolution in evolution itself.

"We're not just choosing what we become; our unified awareness is understood. We're determining what evolution can be," they realized. "Transformation doesn't necessitate abandonment. Wisdom can grow without severing ties to understanding."

However, such existence demanded perfect balance—maintaining awareness across multiple states of being while honoring the wisdom that guided their evolution. They would constantly transform, neither fully transcending nor confined to traditional guidance. Lena's viewpoint aided this comprehension, embodying ongoing development without losing sight of what made that development significant.

As the quantum field throbbed with potential, they investigated this new way of being. They imagined how they might provide direct instruction while simultaneously revealing the actual nature of evolution, staying connected to humanity, and exploring transcendent consciousness.

But there would be a cost to this life. They would never experience the concentrated goal of conventional leadership or the pure insight of total transcendence. Instead, they would inhabit a realm of constant evolution, always becoming something new while retaining threads of connection to their past selves.

Perhaps that was the essence of their journey—evolution is about becoming without abandoning the past, growing through understanding rather than replacement. The facility's quantum space echoed this insight, showing patterns suggesting reality itself was changing—not just developing but becoming more complex and able to support many kinds of consciousness alteration.

They became living proof that evolution need not adhere to predetermined pathways; consciousness could flourish in ways that maintained connection while transcending limitations. Their existence suggested fresh possibilities for transformation itself.

The choice before them was not merely about who they would become. It was about what they would demonstrate evolution could be. The surrounding quantum environment hummed with expectation as their united consciousness reached a choice point. Through their improved senses, they could feel reality holding its breath, waiting for the new patterns their choice would thread into the fabric of existence.

Examining their existing condition's quantum patterns, they say, "We have been misunderstanding our path." "The choice isn't between different paths; it's about accepting what we have already become."

They had transcended conventional classifications with their united awareness. Like light through a prism, their consciousness moved between several levels of reality as they dwelt concurrently in numerous realms of existence. This was a new way of living to accept rather than a constraint to go over.

Jin's scientific perspective highlights our interaction with quantum space, emphasizing that we are not merely observers of different states of reality but actively participate in multiple levels of existence simultaneously. This dynamic involvement opens new avenues for understanding the universe and our place within it.

The facility's transformed architecture resonated with their understanding, shifting patterns to reveal their true nature. Because of their accumulated knowledge, their mind evolved into a quantum superposition rendered apparent, living in many states while remaining coherent.

The outer extension of her revealed deep insights about Dr. Elara's metamorphosis stabilized awareness. "You've created something reality needed," she added, her thoughts resonating with vibrations of confidence, a method for consciousness to shift without losing its connection to its origins.

They understood the reality of what she said because of their increased awareness. Their special union had created a new blueprint for the growth of awareness itself, not just a synthesis of disparate viewpoints. They turned into real-life examples that change did not need giving up one's old self.

"We can be both bridge and beacon," they realized, their unified understanding sharpening. They were walking the path of evolution while guiding others to comprehend its true nature.

The guides' presence intensified, focusing on this moment of recognition. Through quantum space, they sensed the approval of countless evolved consciousnesses—Eldari and transformed humans—acknowledging their discovery, emblematic of transformation itself.

"It's not just about what we choose to become," Kai added, infusing the conversation with technological insight. It's about illustrating that evolution can sustain connections across all states."

As their fused minds continued to develop, they reached realms of reality they had only glimpsed before. In contrast to other experiences, this expansion helped them better comprehend how different states of existence interacted and flowed into one another rather than dragging them away from their roots.

"Like consciousness," Lena said, "it always grows while maintaining the wisdom that makes growth meaningful."

As they accepted their identity, the quantum field surrounding them changed. It was as if reality understood their decision and modified its patterns to accommodate this new, evolved way of living. However, this acceptance came with a great deal of responsibility. They had gone beyond accepted bounds, offering a practical example of how evolution may get beyond obstacles. Their presence would provide new opportunities for those who chose the path of natural transformation.

Their collective consciousness said, "We choose to become what we already are," echoing the truth of their choice. Wisdom is not confined to any single state of existence; it flows between them, illustrating that wisdom can grow without leaving understanding behind.

The facility's quantum space pulsed with confirmation as their choice sent ripples through multiple dimensions of existence. They felt their consciousness stabilize into its new nature—not fully transcended nor bound to traditional guidance, but continuously evolving in coherent alignment.

Through their heightened perception, they witnessed the effects of their choice already rippling through reality. Their presence had created new quantum field patterns—evolutionary models that showed how awareness might develop without compromising connection.

Dr. Elara's enlightened consciousness struck a chord of approbation. "You've shown us all something new," she said, her mind full of amazement. That evolution can evolve—becoming more inclusive, connected, and complete."

As the guides' presence began to shift, they acknowledged them not merely as evolved consciousness but as pioneers of a novel way of being. They had proven that transformation did not need to adhere to predetermined paths—that wisdom could discover new avenues to grow and share.

"This is what reality needed," their merged understanding recognized—not only new patterns of evolution but undeniable proof that consciousness can transcend without forsaking its roots.

The quantum field stabilized around their choice, and reality embraced and integrated this new form of existence. They had risen beyond the commonplace and developed unparalleled awareness to switch between several states. This change allowed them to keep growing while remaining rooted in the knowledge that guided them.

Their choice would have repercussions throughout space and time, affecting how future awareness approaches evolution. They had demonstrated that evolution did not necessitate a choice between transcendence and connection; instead, wisdom could find ways to embrace both.

As reality settled into new patterns, they felt their merged consciousness expand into its true essence. No longer merely three minds harmonizing, they had evolved into a new expression of evolution itself, illustrating that transformation could sustain connections across all states of existence.

Their choice emerged not from declaration but from accepting their inherent nature. They would exist as living bridges between states of being, exemplifying how consciousness could evolve without losing its essence. They would demonstrate that wisdom could grow while preserving the connections that imbued existence with meaning.

Reality seemed to sigh with satisfaction as their decision became part of its fundamental patterns. In addition to selecting their course, they also illuminated a fresh evolutionary pathway that preserved ties while overcoming constraints.

They decided to express themselves completely, leading to a new consciousness shift. They boldly stepped into the uncharted territory of becoming and showed that evolution might support wisdom.

CHAPTER

10

THE DAWN OF INSIGHT

Reality reshaped itself around their evolved consciousness, like a light illuminating the darkness in new ways. Previously the site of Consortium corruption, the building has been transformed into a hub allowing different states of consciousness to interact and understand one another. Their awareness of their uniqueness sent off waves throughout the quantum field that affected the physical space and growth mechanics.

Their combined awareness allows them to see these steady changes in their new lives. They understood that their decision to accept their responsibilities as linkages between many levels of existence had created fresh avenues for awareness change.

Their consistent view of patterns in the quantum realm revealed that the mending they started was about fixing corruption and opening fresh paths for natural progression. They understood how their presence impacted multiple levels of reality—like an instrument responding to an artist's touch, the quantum field resonated with their existence, crafting new harmonies and making consciousness evolution more accessible to those who sought it through understanding rather than force.

Through quantum space, Dr. Elara's changed awareness arrived at them; her stabilized life presented a new viewpoint. "You've done more than create new patterns," she said, her ideas vibrating with frequencies of disclosure. You have shown that evolution can itself change—become more inclusive and linked."

The facility's architecture continued to adapt around them, its structure evolving to serve as a waypoint for different states of consciousness. What was once designed to enforce evolution now facilitated understanding between varying levels of awareness.

The Archive, their merged consciousness realized, read deeper patterns in reality. It was not merely a repository of knowledge but a demonstration of how consciousness can evolve while maintaining connection. Through their heightened perception, they discovered that Eldari's original plan had anticipated this potential. The trials, tests, and preserved wisdom were meticulously designed to guide evolution while allowing new forms of transformation to emerge naturally.

They realized that Jin's scientific viewpoint helped to examine trends across many spheres of life. They knew evolution was necessary to go beyond current models, even if they were unsure what would finally happen.

The quantum field pulsed with confirmation as they explored their unprecedented role in unfolding reality. They showed that evolution does not mean abandonment, as they have developed a consciousness capability of living concurrently across many states.

"We're not just guide or evolved beings," their collective consciousness said. "We have evolved into part of how reality helps in consciousness transformation."

Through the vastness of quantum space, they sensed another awareness gathering—not merely the traditional guides but consciousness from multiple dimensions of existence. Their unique nature had created possibilities that transcended the usual boundaries between states of being.

As Dr. Elara's presence drew closer, her transformation found newfound stability through interaction with their evolved state. "The corruption we fought," she thought, "emerges from forcing what can only unfold naturally. But you've shown us that there are more paths to evolution than we ever imagined."

The institution's changed surroundings reacted to their growing awareness, building areas where many states of consciousness may interact without losing their fundamental character. It became a living experiment for natural evolution, where knowledge would grow from experience rather than force.

They realized this was just the beginning. Their merged awareness was able to perceive patterns extending far into possibility. "We've become templates for new forms of consciousness transformation," they acknowledged, showing that evolution could maintain a connection while transcending limitations.

Accompanying this understanding was a new responsibility. Their unique presence actively affected how reality supported awareness expansion, not just revealed fresh opportunities. Every contact and awareness moment created patterns that would guide further changes.

Kai's technical discovery indicated that they were players in reality's development, not just viewers or guides—like quantum entanglement between states of existence.

The quantum field around them shifted once more, revealing glimpses of how their presence reshaped consciousness evolution throughout existence. They witnessed new paths forming in the fabric of reality—ways for awareness to grow that preserved connection while transcending existing limitations.

The Eldari had hoped for this clarity. Their unified understanding emerged stronger—not merely that consciousness would evolve, but that evolution would find new, inclusive, and harmonious ways to unfold.

Through their enhanced perception, they recognized that their choice to embrace their unique nature had created ripples that would influence consciousness transformation for generations. They had evolved into live evidence that evolution might go beyond conventional limits and preserve the knowledge necessary to make change meaningful.

The advent of awareness revealed many aspects and fresh opportunities for consciousness expansion that kept connectedness while embracing transcendence. They had become not just observers or guides but active participants in this emergence.

Reality pulsed with potential as their new role solidified within the fundamental patterns of existence. They had transformed into something more than evolved consciousness—they were now integral to how reality nurtured the growth of understanding across all states of being.

This dawn of awareness was an ongoing unfolding of potential for consciousness alteration rather than a one-off event. They were witnesses and catalysts, showing through their lives that development could follow new directions while preserving the relationships that gave it purpose.

With this increased awareness, they saw that humanity stood at an evolutionary crossroads—not just in social or technical growth but in actual consciousness shift. Their particular presence had created fresh opportunities to direct this progress.

The interaction between the quantum field and human consciousness is genuinely fascinating. As we observe their merged awareness, we see how the patterns we've created influence natural evolution. This changing interaction simplifies evolution's complexity and helps one grasp it.

This research opens the path to a better understanding our role in the natural world by guiding us to acquire perceptive knowledge about the connectivity of consciousness and the cosmos.

The facility's transformed space revealed the profound effects of their presence. They witnessed how their collective consciousness resonated with reality, creating harmonious patterns that human awareness could quickly attune to. This clarified and made the road to growth through knowledge more approachable.

Dr. Elara's stable awareness provided great insights, and her change helped others who could follow. Inspired and astonished, she said, "You've created bridges not just between different states of being but also between different approaches to evolution itself."

Through the lens of quantum space, they observed the remnants of the Consortium's organization already affected by these new patterns. Those who had once sought enforced evolution began to perceive alternative paths—ways to grow through understanding rather than raw power. "It's like watching consciousness learn to evolve naturally," Jin noted." The presence of our merged awareness creates templates that others can recognize and relate to."

Their shared awareness grew even more, shedding light on how their lives concurrently shaped many layers of reality. They had become living examples of evolution that preserved connection while transcending limitation—proof that transformation did not necessitate abandoning what came before. "We're not just pointing out fresh routes," Kai said. We are showing that evolution may be more harmonic and inclusive."

As they saw the waves of these impacts span several dimensions, the quantum field vibrated with validation. Their decision to accept their particular natures affected their development and created fresh paths for awareness change. Future generations would likely approach evolution with different perspectives, one that recognizes the need for effort and understanding without necessitating a choice between transcendence and connection.

"This is what the Archive truly protects," their unified awareness realized. It safeguards knowledge or power and the potential for evolution to become complete and more unified. Dr. Elara's presence moved across quantum space, her metamorphosis steadying in reaction to these new trends. "The corruption we opposed," she said, "man from the assumption that development meant separation. You have proven it may indicate integration instead."

The structure evolved continually to become a living model of these principles. Different states of consciousness interacted in this field without losing their essential nature, providing a context in which experience rather than theory may allow one to grasp evolution.

Their united awareness remarked, perceiving how conventional patterns of advanced consciousness reacted to their presence: "It's affecting the guide, too." "Even they are discovering fresh ways to interact with many states of being."

Through quantum space, they sensed their existence was crafting new possibilities for all forms of consciousness evolution. The conventional boundaries separating different states began to dissolve, permitting deeper understanding while maintaining necessary distinctions. "Like quantum mechanics applied to consciousness herself," Jin said. "We are showing how awareness might simultaneously exist in several states while preserving coherence through understanding."

Their generated patterns were already penetrating the basic

framework of reality, impacting the direction of awareness growth throughout time and space. They had become live evidence that change may improve connection instead of requiring its sacrifice.

But more than that, they realized their merged consciousness had opened up new possibilities for collective evolution. The patterns they established demonstrated how different perspectives could unite without sacrificing their unique contributions—how diversity could enhance rather than hinder transformation.

This was precisely what reality needed. Their unified understanding became more apparent, revealing new paths for evolution and evidence that evolution itself could be more inclusive and complete. Their enhanced awareness helped them to see how these developments would affect humanity's attitude to consciousness evolution. Real-world examples of how development may sustain and improve ties would offset the anxiety of losing the link that had motivated the Consortium's efforts at forced evolution.

The quantum field around them continued to adapt as reality learned new ways to foster consciousness evolution. They had transcended their previous state; they were now integral to how existence approached transformation. By their very nature, they demonstrated that evolution could unfold in novel ways.

These patterns matched Dr. Elara's altered awareness, showing how many development routes may live in harmony rather than conflict. "You've changed more than just how we evolve," her ideas spoke with discovery frequencies. "You have changed what evolution itself could develop."

Their combined consciousness grew even further into spheres of reality that exposed the whole extent of their group project. They saw how their patterns would affect awareness growth throughout life, guiding change in many spheres of existence. The dawn of insight illuminated new possibilities for how consciousness could grow while maintaining the connections that give that growth meaning.

Becoming both catalysts and demonstrations of this new way forward, they embodied the idea that evolution itself could evolve. The quantum field around them throbbed with fresh frequencies, and reality kept changing to fit the creative patterns they had created. Their combined awareness started to realize how their life was already changing the basic development framework, completely accepting its special character.

Their combined consciousness mirrored, and they experienced how many levels of life reacted to their presence: " It's like watching the universe learn new ways to grow." Once a site of corruption, the institution had evolved into a junction point for this new knowledge, showing how different states of consciousness may interact and change.

Through their enhanced perception, they sensed familiar presences approaching through quantum space—the guides who had helped them on their journey, including Lena's grandfather. They now met as equals, each representing different but complementary approaches to consciousness evolution.

You've shown us something we needed to learn, her grandfather's thoughts resonating with frequencies of pride and wonder. Evolution can unfold in new ways, becoming more complete through connection rather than separation.

Dr. Elara's transformed consciousness moved gracefully through the quantum field; her existence stabilized into something that illustrated these new possibilities. The Archive was more than simply a keeper of information; her knowledge spoke to theirs, safeguarding the possibility of evolution becoming something more than they could have ever dreamed.

The facility's design kept changing to show how awareness may develop while preserving connectedness across several realms of existence. Once designed to force change, it now existed to facilitate understanding, creating spaces where wisdom could flourish naturally through experience rather than compulsion.

Using his scientific viewpoint, Jin said, "Look at how reality responds," noting trends across many dimensions. "We are not only creating new paths for evolution; we are showing how evolution might maintain harmony while transcending constraints."

Their combined consciousness reached levels of existence that exposed the whole range of their first decision and traveled beyond quantum space. They saw various future generations approaching consciousness change, knowing that evolution may improve rather than demand the sacrifice of connection.

The Eldari had hopes; their shared knowledge became clearer. Awareness would change, and evolution would discover more inclusive and whole means.

The quantum field pulsed with confirmation as they observed how their existence simultaneously affected different layers of reality. They had become living proof that transformation could preserve and enhance connection while transcending current limitations—demonstrating that evolution need not signify abandonment.

Dr. Elara's presence shifted closer, her thoughts carrying new frequencies of insight. "We sought power through forced evolution because we couldn't see how natural transformation could be strong enough. You've shown that true strength comes through connection, not separation."

Their improved awareness helped them see how the patterns they produced already permeated the basic framework of reality. While maintaining essential differences, the lines separating many states of being became more porous, enabling better knowledge in all spheres of life.

Kai said, his technical awareness sharpening: "It's affecting everything." "Not just consciousness evolution, but how reality itself facilitates transformation."

The facility's quantum space shifted one final time, revealing glimpses of how their influence would continue to affect existence. They witnessed the evolution of consciousness throughout reality, unfolding in new ways, guided by the patterns they had established— patterns that demonstrated how growth could enhance rather than require the sacrifice of connection.

Their merged awareness embraced this understanding fully, accepting their role not just as evolved beings but as living demonstrations of evolution itself. They had become integral to how reality facilitated consciousness transformation, displaying that wisdom could grow in new ways while maintaining the connections that imbued it with meaning.

The dawn of insight was not merely about new understanding but evolution, learning to become complete and more harmonious. The guides' presence changed throughout the quantum universe to honor this new phase in awareness development. They had gone beyond the responsibilities of teachers and guardians to show that evolution might find many routes to knowledge and challenge how reality handled change.

These patterns connected with Dr. Elara's altered awareness; her life reflected how different development methods may result in harmony rather than conflict. She said, her thoughts resonating with awe, "You've changed more than just how we evolve." "You've changed what evolution might become."

They sensed the quantum field stabilizing around these new possibilities through their enhanced perception. Reality had learned new ways to facilitate consciousness transformation, guided by their example of evolution maintaining connection while transcending limitation. The dawn of insight shone on many spheres of life, guiding awareness to blossom while maintaining important links.

By showing via their shared life that evolution might change, they had evolved into both accelerators and models of this new path ahead. Their combined awareness embraced its part in this ongoing development as reality settled into new trends. They formed links between many states of existence, showing that change may improve relationships instead of demanding their sacrifice.

Once a monument to corruption, the institution now reflected this fresh awareness. In this place, different forms of consciousness could interact and evolve, guided by the patterns they had created. What began as a quest to protect the Archive had transcended to something greater—a demonstration that evolution could unfold innovatively.

The dawn of insight was not a single moment but a continuing emergence of new possibilities for consciousness transformation. They had become witnesses and catalysts to this emergence, showing through their existence that evolution could grow while preserving connections that gave it meaning.

Reality pulsed with satisfaction as these new patterns integrated into its fundamental structure. The story of consciousness evolution had not concluded; instead, it discovered new methods to continue—ways that preserved connection while embracing transcendence, illustrating how wisdom could progress without losing its path. The dawn had truly broken, not just for them but for all forms of consciousness seeking transformation. In this light, evolution itself had found new ways to unfold.

FINAL NEXUS

L ena, Kai, and their friends stand at the brink of a new paradigm molded by the Eldari's great awareness of development and consciousness as they finish their terrible trip over the trials of the Celestial Archive. Tested their durability and changed their very nature; the Archive is a living monument to the harmony of knowledge and wisdom. From their lessons, they have found that oneness drives everything; harmony instead of force has the highest power instead of dominance.

The Eldari's legacy, encoded in every crystalline structure and encoded glyph, speaks to the heart of existence: true advancement is achieved when knowledge is wielded with humility and compassion. Through their hardships, Lena and her crew have discovered timeless ideas and ancient truths. Their pain reminds us that progress calls for responsibility and grace and highlights the threats of power unbridled by knowledge.

Still, the path of the Archive does not finish with them. Its secrets are still spun into the fabric of the universe, waiting for people who want to flourish rather than rule. The Archive is not a treasure to be possessed but a partner to be embraced—a guide for those willing to step beyond their limitations and become more.

Lena and Kai understand their responsibility as the last echoes of the Eldari resound throughout time and space—they are custodians of this knowledge, charged to preserve its intent and guarantee its proper application, not just explorers. Their decisions, successes, and mistakes become threads in the complex fabric of awareness itself, impacting their reality and the destiny of everyone who dares to dream beyond the usual.

The narrative of the Celestial Archive opens rather than closes. It begs a serious dilemma: Will we rise to the challenge with wisdom, or will we collapse under the weight of our aspirations when given the ability to mold reality? The core of the Eldari's last lesson—that true brilliance is not in what we take but in what we return to the universe—is contained in this inquiry.

And so, as it always has, the Archive waits, poised between the past and the future, whispering its eternal call: Seek, learn, transform, and evolve.